This book
belongs to:

ALSO BY JUDITH VIORST

Lulu and the Brontosaurus

Lulu Walks the Dogs

The Tenth Good Thing About Barney

*Alexander and the Terrible, Horrible,
No Good, Very Bad Day*

*My Mama Says There Aren't Any Zombies,
Ghosts, Vampires, Creatures, Demons,
Monsters, Fiends, Goblins, or Things*

Rosie and Michael

*Alexander, Who Used to
Be Rich Last Sunday*

The Good-Bye Book

*Alexander, Who's Not (Do You Hear Me?
I Mean It!) Going to Move*

Earrings!

Super-Completely and Totally the Messiest

Just in Case

*If I Were in Charge of the World and Other
Worries: Poems for Children and Their
Parents*

*Sad Underwear and Other Complications:
More Poems for Children and Their Parents*

LULU

and Her Mischievous Collection

JUDITH VIORST
illustrated by LANE SMITH & KEVIN CORNELL

Atheneum Books for Young Readers

NEW YORK • LONDON • TORONTO • SYDNEY • NEW DELHI

Contents

LULU
and the
Brontosaurus

JUDITH VIORST

illustrated by LANE SMITH

Atheneum Books for Young Readers

NEW YORK • LONDON • TORONTO • SYDNEY • NEW DELHI

These titles were previously published individually.

atheneum

ATHENEUM BOOKS FOR YOUNG READERS
An imprint of Simon & Schuster Children's Publishing Division
1230 Avenue of the Americas, New York, New York 10020

For information about special discounts for bulk purchases, please contact Simon & Schuster Special Sales at 1-866-506-1949 or business@simonandschuster.com.

The Simon & Schuster Speakers Bureau can bring authors to your live event. For more information or to book an event, contact the Simon & Schuster Speakers Bureau at 1-866-248-3049 or visit our website at www.simonspeakers.com.

The text for this book is set in Officina Sans.

The illustrations for this book are rendered in pencil on pastel paper.

Manufactured in the United States of America

0321 FFG

First bindup proprietary edition March 2021

10 9 8 7 6 5 4 3 2 1

Library of Congress Cataloging-in-Publication Data
Lulu and the Brontosaurus
Viorst, Judith.
Lulu and the brontosaurus / Judith Viorst ; illustrated by Lane Smith. — 1st ed.
p. cm.
Summary: Lulu's parents refuse to give in when she demands a brontosaurus for her birthday and so she sets out to find her own, but while the brontosaurus she finally meets approves of pets, he does not intend to be Lulu's.
ISBN 978-1-4169-9961-4 (hardcover)
[1. Behavior—Fiction. 2. Apatosaurus—Fiction. 3. Pets—Fiction. 4. Birthdays—Fiction.]
I. Smith, Lane, ill. II. Title.
PZ7.V816Lul 2010
[Fic]—dc22
2009031664
ISBN 978-1-4169-9963-8 (eBook)
ISBN 978-1-6659-0021-8 (Costco proprietary edition)

BOOK DESIGN BY MOLLY LEACH

For Nathaniel Redding Gwadz Viorst
and Benjamin Carlo Gwadz Viorst,
who helped me write this story
—J. V.

For Molly
—L. S.

OKAY! *All right! You don't*

I know that people and dinosaurs have never lived on Earth at the same time. And *I know* that dinosaurs aren't living now. I even also know that paleontologists (folks who study dinosaurs) decided that a dinosaur that was once called a brontosaurus (a very nice name) shouldn't be called brontosaurus anymore, and

have to tell me! **I know!**

changed it to apatosaurus
(a kind of ugly name). But since
I'm the person writing this story,
I get to choose what I write, and
I'm writing about a girl and a
B R O N T O S A U R U S.
So if you don't want to read this
book, you can close it up right
now—you won't hurt my
feelings. And if you still want
to read it, here goes:

chapter one

There once was a girl named Lulu, and she was a pain. She wasn't a pain in the elbow. She wasn't a pain in the knee. She was a pain—a very big pain—in the

b u t t .

Now, Lulu was an only child, and her mom and her dad gave her everything she wanted. And guess what? Lulu wanted EVERYTHING. Tons of candy. Tons of toys. Tons of watching tons of cartoons on TV. And if her mom and her dad ever said (and they hardly ever said it), "Sorry, darling, we think you've had enough," Lulu would screech till the lightbulbs burst and throw herself down on the floor, and then she would kick her heels and wave her arms. And pretty soon her mom and her dad would say, "Well, just this once," and let her have whatever it was she wanted.

chapter two

Two weeks before Lulu's birthday, she announced to her mom and her dad that she wanted a brontosaurus for her b-day present. What did she say? What? A brontosaurus? Yes, she wanted a brontosaurus for a pet. At first Lulu's mom and her dad just thought she was making a little joke. And then they saw— oh, horrors!—that she was serious.

They patiently explained that a brontosaurus is a quite enormous dinosaur who lives in forests, not in people's houses.

(Is that where a brontosaurus would live? In a forest? I'm afraid that I'm not absolutely sure. But since I'm the person writing this story, I'm putting this brontosaurus in a forest, along with a lot of other wild beasts that I'm absolutely sure did not live on Earth when dinosaurs were there.)

Anyway, Lulu's mom and her dad continued explaining to her, although a brontosaurus is into eating plants, not animals (including human animals like Lulu), and although it is cute (in a long-necked, pinheaded way), it is much too huge and too wild to be a good pet.

A dog,
a cat,
a goldfish,
a bird,
a gerbil,
a guinea pig, yes.

A brontosaurus?

Definitely no.

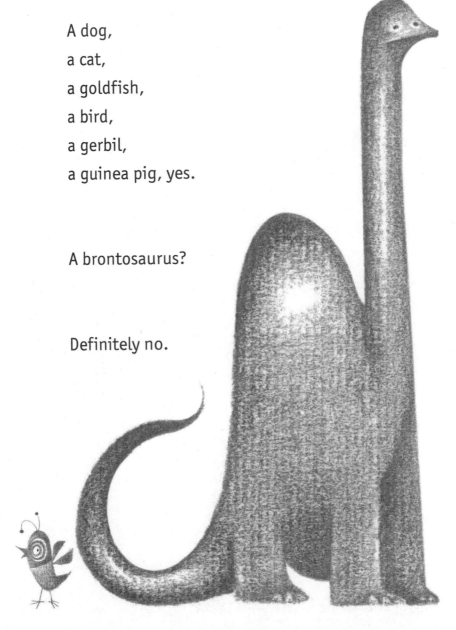

chapter three

No? Her mom and her dad were telling Lulu no? Lulu wasn't used to hearing no. And she hated—she really hated—hearing no. To show how much she hated it, she screeched and screeched and screeched till all the lightbulbs in the living room burst. "I WANT A BRONTOSAURUS FOR MY BIRTHDAY PRESENT," she said in between screeches.

"I WANT A BRONTOSAURUS FOR A PET."

"Well, maybe we could get you a nice pet rabbit," said her mom.

"Or even," said her dad, "a nice pet rat."

"Nonononononono!" screeched Lulu.

"I WANT A BRONTOSAURUS FOR A PET."

Then she threw herself down on the floor and kicked her heels and waved her arms and screeched some more.

chapter four

Four days, eight days, ten days, twelve days passed. Lulu kept saying, "I WANT A BRONTOSAURUS." Her mom and her dad just kept on saying no. Lulu kept screeching and throwing herself on the floor and kicking her heels and waving her arms. Lulu's mom and her dad kept saying no. Until finally, on the thirteenth day, the day before Lulu's birthday, right after lunch, Lulu said to her mom and her dad, "Okay then, foo on you." (She had terrible manners.) "If you aren't going to get me a brontosaurus, I'm going out and getting one for myself."

Lulu packed a small suitcase, said good-bye to her mom and her dad, and walked out the door.

And they let her go! Partly because they thought she'd change her mind and come running back home in about two minutes. And partly because it was nice to not have her screeching and kicking and waving and being a pain.

"Let's have a cup of tea and a couple of cookies," Lulu's mom said to her dad.

"Excellent idea," her dad replied.

So they went into the kitchen and started munching on some cookies and sipping tea. And pretty soon they'd forgotten all about Lulu.

chapter five

But Lulu hadn't forgotten that she was going to get herself a brontosaurus. And luckily for Lulu, there was a great big forest not too far from her house. The animals in that forest had never bothered anybody, because nobody had ever bothered them. But—watch out, creatures!—here came Lulu, trudging through the forest, swinging her small suitcase back and forth, and—in a quite loud voice that was sure to wake the napping animals from their naps—singing this song:

I'm gonna, I'm gonna, I'm gonna,

gonna get

A bronto-bronto-bronto
Brontosaurus for a pet.

I'm gonna, I'm gonna,
I'm gonna, gonna get

A bronto-bronto-bronto
Brontosaurus for a pet.

The forest that Lulu was trudging through was overgrown with trees whose branches scratched her face and whose roots she tripped over. But Lulu hardly noticed, because she was thinking just one thought, and you know what that was.

So on she went, swinging her suitcase
and singing her song too loud and
annoying all the creatures in the forest,
and being the same big pain out there
that she was back home in her house,

until . . .

Slithering down from the branch of a
tree came a long, fat, brown-black snake,
who had been peacefully snoozing till
Lulu woke him up. Sleepy and grumpy
and hissing an exceedingly nasty hiss,
he wrapped himself around Lulu, around
and around and tighter and tighter, and
told her she'd really be sorry that she had
awakened him.

"I'm going to squeeze you dead," he said.

(Okay, so snakes don't talk. But in my story they do.)

And Lulu said, "Not if I squeeze you deader."

So Lulu squeezed the snake—hard!— and the snake yelled, "Ow!" and quickly unwrapped himself from Lulu. And Lulu, wiping some snake sweat from the palms of her snake-squeezing hands, went on trudging deeper into the forest.

chapter six

I'm gonna, I'm gonna,
I'm gonna, gonna get
A bronto-bronto-bronto
Brontosaurus for a pet.
I'm gonna, I'm gonna,
I'm gonna, gonna get
A bronto-bronto-bronto
Brontosaurus for a pet.

Singing her brontosaurus song in a louder and louder voice, Lulu was waking up nappers all over the forest. Some were annoyed. Some were extremely annoyed. Among the extremely annoyed was a silky, slinky lady tiger, who yawned and stretched and rubbed her bright green eyes, and then, with a ferocious roar, sprung out from behind some trees and pounced on Lulu.

"You're a big pain," the tiger said, "so I'm going to eat you up for my afternoon snack."

"Uh-uh," said Lulu. "I'm bonking you on the head." And swinging, swinging with all her might, Lulu bonked the tiger with her suitcase.

The tiger yelled, "Ow!" and fell down in a pitiful black-and-orange-striped heap on the forest floor. Lulu brushed off a few tiger hairs that were stuck to the side of her tiger-bonking suitcase and went on trudging deeper into the forest.

chapter seven

As the afternoon turned into late afternoon and then into early evening, Lulu trudged ever deeper into the forest. When she felt hungry, she opened her suitcase and took out a pickle sandwich.

When she felt cold, she took out a
sweater and socks. And when it got
buggy, she opened her suitcase and
took out some bug spray and sprayed.
She was feeling a little tired, but she
kept trudging, and swinging her suitcase,
and singing her song.

I'm gonna, I'm gonna,

I'm gonna, gonna get

A bronto-bronto-bronto

Brontosaurus for a pet.

I'm gonna, I'm gonna,

I'm gonna, gonna get

A bronto-bronto-bronto

Brontosaurus for a pet.

Now, a big black bear who liked listening to the music that insects make in the early evening couldn't hear their song because Lulu's was louder. Plus, a lot of the insects were deader because Lulu kept on spraying them with her spray. This made him mad. Then madder. Then madder than that. He growled a thunderous growl, and then he lumbered heavily down the forest path and stood on his two hind legs in front of Lulu. Waving a big claw-y paw in her face, he said, "You're interrupting my favorite program." (Please don't give me an argument. In my story, bears are allowed to have favorite programs.) "So I'm going to scratch you to pieces with my claws."

Lulu glared at the big black bear and put her hands on her hips. "Nobody's scratching *me*," she told the bear. Then she jumped—as high as she possibly could—in the air. Then she landed—as hard as she possibly could—on his foot.

The bear yelled, "Ow!" and went limping away, as fast as a bear could limp with one stomped foot. And after shaking some broken bear toenails off the bottoms of her bear-stomping shoes, Lulu went trudging deeper into the forest.

chapter eight

Lulu was now in the deepest, darkest, quietest part of the forest. It was getting quite late and she was getting quite tired. She took her sleeping bag out of her suitcase, spread it on the ground, and lay down to sleep. But before she slept, she sang her song once more.

I'm gonna, I'm gonna,

I'm gonna, gonna get

A bronto-bronto-bronto

Brontosaurus for a pet.

I'm gonna, I'm gonna,

I'm gonna, gonna get

A bronto-bronto-bronto

Brontosaurus for a pet.

Actually, she never even got to sing
the last line because, before she could
get to it, she was sleeping.

chapter eight
and one half

At dawn Lulu woke to the sound of birds calling to one another, and the dusky-musky smell of the forest floor, and the feel of a gentle late-summer breeze blowing across her face, and the taste (because she hadn't bothered to brush her teeth before bedtime) of yesterday's pickle sandwich. She also woke to the sight of something so huge, so enormous, so utterly gigantic that she thought—no, she was sure—that she was still dreaming. It looked like a mountain, except this mountain had legs, a very long neck, and a very small head. It was (as I'm sure you've already figured out) the brontosaurus that Lulu had been searching for.

chapter nine

Lulu closed, then opened, then closed, then opened her eyes again, and decided she wasn't dreaming after all. She quickly climbed out of her sleeping bag and announced to the brontosaurus, "It's my birthday today and—just in time!—I've found you."

"No, *I've* found *you*," the brontosaurus told Lulu. "And I'd like to wish you a very happy birthday."

"Oh, it will be very happy," Lulu said
to the brontosaurus, "because you"—
she patted his ankle, because his ankle
was as high as she could reach—"you
are the pet I'm getting for my birthday."

The brontosaurus bent down his
neck so his face was close to Lulu's.
He looked at her back to front and head
to toes, sniffing at her carefully with
his brontosaurus nose and making a
rumbling noise (nobody knows how
dinosaurs sound, but in my story they
rumble) and slowly nodding, nodding
his pinheaded head.

"A pet," he said to Lulu, after he'd nodded for a while, "is a very good thing."

"A very, very good thing," Lulu replied. She opened up her suitcase and went digging around inside and pulled out a white leather collar, which she fastened around the brontosaurus's neck.

"Now I'll just attach this leash"—she dug some more and found a long, long leash in her suitcase—"and take you home with me."

Lulu attached the leash to the collar, feeling so pleased with herself that she sang a whole new brontosaurus song.

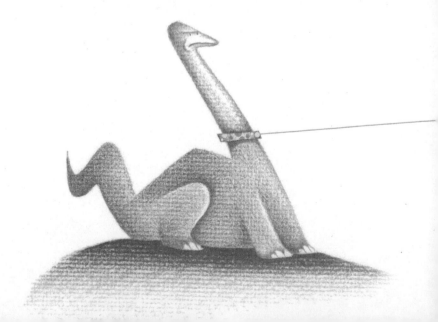

I got it! I got it! I got
What I wanted to get,
A bronto-bronto-bronto
Brontosaurus for a pet.
I got it! I got it! I got
What I wanted to get,
A bronto-bronto-bronto
Brontosaurus for a pet.

She would have kept feeling pleased
with herself, except now the brontosaurus
was shaking his head. And now, in his
rumbling voice, he was saying, "No." He
was saying no and shaking his head till
the collar and leash flew off. "No," he
said, "I don't wish to be your pet."

Lulu, remember, hated hearing no. She
really, really hated hearing no. So she
screeched till all the birds fled from the
trees, and then she threw herself down on
the forest floor, and then she kicked her
heels and waved her arms.

The brontosaurus waited patiently, without saying one more word, until she had stopped with the screeching and kicking and waving. "Finished now?" he quite politely asked.

"Maybe I am," Lulu said. "And maybe I'm not. It all depends"—and here she shook a finger right in the brontosaurus's face; this girl was a pain, but she wasn't a scaredy-cat—"it all depends on whether you stop saying no and start saying yes to being my pet."

The brontosaurus shook his head no some more. Lulu thought about screeching and so forth some more. But instead she said, in a very snippy voice, "Now listen here, you were the one who said to me just a minute ago that—and I quote—'A PET IS A VERY GOOD THING.'"

"That's what I said," the brontosaurus admitted.

"So what," Lulu asked, "is your problem, Mr. B?"

"No problem," he answered. "Just a misunderstanding. Because when I said that a pet is a very good thing, I didn't mean I wanted to be *your* pet. I meant that *you'd* be a very good pet for *me*."

chapter ten

Lulu's eyes were two round Os of amazement. She tried to speak, but at first no words came out. Then finally she was able to say, in a squeaky, amazed kind of voice, "I don't think I heard what I think I just heard, Mr. B."

"You did indeed," the brontosaurus replied.

"Well, if I did"—Lulu's voice was back to being its old bossy self again—"well, if I did, I've got some news for you. A person HAS a pet. An animal IS a pet. A person can't be an animal's pet, E V E R ."

"And I have some news for you," the brontosaurus said to Lulu, except that he spoke more politely than Lulu had done. "You're about to be the first person—ever—to be an animal's pet. Congratulations and, once again, happy birthday."

He reached out a hand (or whatever you want to call it) and gently scooped Lulu off the forest floor.

He then plunked her gently down where his back met his neck. "Hold on tight, little pet," he said to Lulu. "I'll pull off some leaves from the tops of the trees for your breakfast. And then I'm taking you home to live with me."

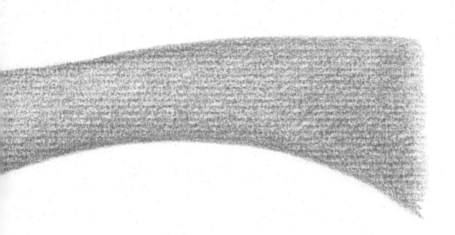

"No!" yelled Lulu. "No! No! No! A billion zillion times no."

"Yes, yes, yes," the brontosaurus replied. "I'll feed you and pat you and play with you and treat you very nicely. And all I'll expect from you is to sit and roll over and fetch a ball and do cute tricks." (What did he think she was, some kind of dog-girl? I really don't know; I can't read a dinosaur's mind.)

Lulu thought about screeching and throwing herself on the forest floor, except that the forest floor was a long way down. She thought about squeezing the dinosaur dead, except that she needed both hands to hang on to his neck. She thought about swinging and swinging her suitcase and bonking him on the head, except that she'd left her suitcase under a tree. And she couldn't stomp on his foot, because his feet were far too far from his back, where he'd plunked her.

Then Lulu started to think that the only thing farther from where the brontosaurus had plunked her was her home, her home where her mom and her dad were waiting, her very own home where no one—not even when she was being a pain (which was most of the time)—had ever, ever expected her to sit and roll over and fetch and do cute tricks.

"I want to go home to *my* house," Lulu told the brontosaurus, then added in a lot-less-bossier voice, "Please let me go back to my house, Mr. B."

This was maybe the very first time in Lulu's entire life that she, without being told, had used the P word. And yet the brontosaurus shook his head no. "Once you get used to it," he kindly told Lulu, "I truly believe that you'll like being a pet."

Lulu imagined being a pet in the house of this brontosaurus and never seeing her mom or her dad again. She imagined eating leaves and doing cute tricks. And she said to herself that if only she could turn today into yesterday, she wouldn't go looking for dinosaurs in the forest and she wouldn't say, "Foo on you" to her mom and her dad.

She was feeling especially sorry that she had ever said, "Foo on you" to her mom and her dad.

chapter eleven

The brontosaurus pulled leaves off the trees and was offering them to Lulu. She grabbed them and threw them angrily away.

"A simple 'no, thank you' will do," the brontosaurus said to Lulu. "And I really liked that 'please' you used before."

"So please please please, let me please go home!" yelled Lulu.

"Your yelling is hurting my ears," said the dinosaur. "But I have to admit that even if you had asked me softly and sweetly, I still would want to keep you here with me. I've been lonely, and a pet is a very good thing."

For hours and hours and hours, from early morning till just past noon, Lulu kept telling the brontosaurus he had to let her go home, and the brontosaurus kept telling Lulu no. He also kept assuring her that he'd do his absolute best to make her happy. He spoke in such a kind and nice and polite and patient voice that after a while Lulu was talking, not yelling. And after a while she was talking softly and sweetly. And pretty soon after that, she started to cry.

Yes, Lulu started to cry. And it wasn't very often that Lulu cried. She'd rather screech till the lightbulbs burst and all of that other stuff, but right now she didn't feel screechy—she felt teary. And so she cried and cried and cried, soaking the brontosaurus with her tears.

He patiently waited as Lulu continued soaking him, and the forest floor, with her tears. He patiently waited some more and then he said, "I'm sorry I'm making you cry, little pet, but I won't be changing my mind. Would you like a tissue?"

Lulu now understood that no matter how hard she cried and how nice this dinosaur was, he was determined to keep her as his pet. And she now understood that if she was determined to NOT be his pet, she would have to escape. She cried just a little bit longer, but while she was crying on the outside, she was—on the inside—making a getaway plan.

Sniffing a watery sniff, Lulu said to the brontosaurus, "Thank you, Mr. B, I do need some tissues. If you'll just let me down on the forest floor for a minute, I'm sure I can find a box of them in my suitcase."

The brontosaurus lowered his head and his neck to the floor of the forest. Lulu slid off, stood up, and smiled a small smile. She walked to her suitcase, opened it, poked around for a while, and found (are you surprised?) a big box of tissues.

But instead of taking the tissues out, she put her sleeping bag in, snapped her suitcase shut, and . . . started running.

The brontosaurus stood stiff and still, as if he'd been glued to the ground. And then he started running after Lulu. But Lulu had darted off the path, into the heart of the forest, into a part of the forest where the trees grew so close together that a creature as huge as this dinosaur could not fit. She zigged and she zagged and she zigged and she zagged through those close-together trees while the brontosaurus looked for spaces to squeeze through.

He was trying his hardest to catch her—
as hard as a mountain-size creature can
try—but she was leaving him farther and
farther behind. "Come back, little pet,
come back," Lulu could hear him calling,
first loudly, then softer and softer. "Come
back, little pet. I know you'll be happy
with me."

"Come back, little pet. . . ." His voice
grew ever softer. And soon she could not
hear his voice anymore.

Since Lulu could not hear his voice
anymore, she stopped running and
started walking. She tromped through
the forest in silence, heading for home.

But she wasn't swinging her suitcase
and she wasn't singing her song, and
although she very much wanted to see
her mom and her dad again, and very
much wanted NOT to be a pet, she felt
kind of bad about the brontosaurus.
(And so do I. Because even though I'm
the person writing this story, I don't
like leaving him all alone, sadly calling,
"Come back, little pet. Come back.")

chapter twelve

But then, after maybe an hour, Lulu suddenly heard a different voice, a not-so-friendly voice, saying, "Hold it right there." And standing up on his two hind legs, and blocking her path through the forest, stood the black bear she had stomped on yesterday.

"*You* hold it right there," said Lulu, "and please"—there was that P word again—"don't keep shaking your claw-y paws at me. If I have to stomp you, I'll stomp you, but I'd really rather not stomp you. I'd rather"—she opened her suitcase and took out a jar of golden honey—"give you this if you'll please get out of my way." (What's going on with Lulu? She'd rather not *stomp* him?)

The bear took the jar of honey, opened the top, dipped in his paw, and slurpily licked it, mumbling something that sort of sounded like "Thank you." Dipping and licking and slurping, he hurried out of Lulu's path. And she continued tromping through the forest.

Until . . . another familiar, another not-too-friendly voice said, "This time I'm eating you before you bonk me." And there was the tiger, the silky, slinky tiger of yesterday, ready to pounce on her.

"Forget the eating and bonking," said Lulu, "and try on this beautiful scarf." She pulled a long, floaty, bright green scarf from her suitcase. "It matches your eyes, and I'll give it to you if you'll please get out of my way." And the tiger, happily wrapping the eye-matching scarf around her black-and-orange-striped neck, growled something that sounded like "Thank you," and slunk away. And Lulu continued tromping through the forest.

Until . . . well, what do you think she met next? A wolf? A giraffe? A lion? Don't be ridiculous. She met—of course she met; what else?—the snake, who was hissing an even nastier hiss than he'd hissed the day before and warning her, "This time *I'll* be the tighter squeezer."

Lulu, looking disgusted, told him, "Nobody's squeezing anybody. All I'm doing is getting home today." Then she reached in her suitcase and pulled out a small flowered rug and explained to the snake, "This is for you if you'll please get out of my way. A soft rug to rest on whenever you feel like resting."

The snake took the rug in his mouth
and tried (at least I think he tried) to say
thank you to Lulu, though it's hard to tell
when a mouth is full of rug. In any case,
he went slithering off wherever a snake
goes slithering. And Lulu continued
tromping through the forest.

chapter thirteen

$\mathcal{H}$ wasn't too much later that Lulu could see that she was nearly out of the forest. She was happy that soon she would be with her mom and her dad. But along with feeling happy, she was also feeling sad when she thought of the brontosaurus she'd left behind. As a matter of fact, she pictured the poor lonely dinosaur so clearly in her mind that it almost seemed he was standing there, just outside of the forest, waiting for her.

AND HE WAS!

Was Lulu shocked? You bet! "What—what—what," she asked, "are you doing here, Mr. B?"

"I found a shortcut," the brontosaurus replied.

Lulu smiled a soft, sweet smile, then shook her head and sighed. And then she said (and even though I'm the person writing this story, I truly don't know why she's saying it in rhyme):

"Please try to understand, Mr. B,
That I cannot be your pet.
Even though you're the nicest
Brontosaurus I ever met.
And if you take me away with you,
I'll keep on running back home—
Every chance that I get."

(Not a bad rhyme, though
that last line's a little lumpy.)

"I already figured that out while I was waiting for you," the brontosaurus told Lulu. "I do understand that you can't be my pet. But please understand that I can't be *your* pet either."

Well, Lulu understood and the brontosaurus understood. It seemed there was only one thing left to do. So they stood there, quietly looking at each other for a moment. And then they did it.

The brontosaurus bent his long neck till his face was close to Lulu's. He kissed her gently on the cheek and said, "Happy birthday, little pet . . . and good-bye."

Lulu put her arms around the brontosaurus's neck. She kissed him gently on his nose and said, "Don't be too lonely, Mr. B . . . and good-bye."

Then she slowly walked down the road that would take her home.

Then he slowly walked down the road that would take him home.

And although Lulu and the brontosaurus remembered each other forever, they never ever saw each other again.

The
(maybe)
End

chapter thirteen

(again)

Wait! I'm really not all that sure about this ending. It may be a little too mushy, a little too sad. But since I'm the person writing this story, I'm writing another ending and you can decide which one you'd rather have:

Well, Lulu understood and the brontosaurus understood that neither of them could be the other's pet. But why should that mean that they had to say good-bye? "Come with me and I'll give you a piece of my birthday cake," said Lulu.

"I'd like that," the dinosaur said. "May I give you a ride?"

And Lulu arrived at her house, riding happily on the back of the brontosaurus.

When her mom and her dad heard the noise of a dinosaur clomping into their yard, they remembered Lulu and they remembered her birthday. Lucky for all, her cake had already been made. "Don't worry. He isn't my pet," Lulu said. "He's only going to stay here for a piece of cake and a glass of lemonade. But he's kind of a lonely guy, and I would like to invite him back for Thanksgiving dinner."

From that time on, the brontosaurus came to Lulu's house for her birthday, Thanksgiving, and the Fourth of July. And sometimes she visited his house, though (since she didn't like eating leaves) she always brought a suitcase of pickle sandwiches. On one very special birthday she not only invited her friend the brontosaurus, but also the snake and the tiger and the bear. And the brontosaurus noticed that whenever Lulu asked anyone for anything, she always said please.

The
End
(maybe)

chapter thirteen
(yet again)

Hmmm. I'm still not totally satisfied. I'm going to try once more, because I think I need to answer certain questions. Like: Were Lulu's mom and her dad worried sick when she didn't come home that night? Had they bought her a present for her birthday? Did she completely stop being a pain and turn into polite? And how did all that stuff fit into her suitcase? I'm going to answer these questions, and when I'm done you will have your choice of *three* different endings.

Well, Lulu understood and the brontosaurus understood that, though they couldn't be pets, they could be friends. So Lulu invited the brontosaurus back to her house for some birthday cake and introduced him to her mom and her dad. They hadn't been waiting and worrying and wondering where she was because they had fallen asleep sipping their tea, and they didn't open their eyes till the brontosaurus, with Lulu riding on his back, came clomp-clomp-clomping into their front yard.

They gave her a silver necklace for her birthday.

She sang them a whole new brontosaurus song:

I *didn't,* I *didn't,*
I didn't, didn't get
A bronto-bronto-bronto
Brontosaurus for a pet.
I *didn't,* I *didn't,*
I didn't, didn't get
A bronto-bronto-bronto
Brontosaurus for a pet.

"It sure looks like you've brought one home," Lulu's mom said to Lulu.

"And we still say no, you can't have one," said her dad. And both of them waited for Lulu to screech and throw herself down on the floor and kick her heels and wave her arms in the air.

Except she didn't.

"What happened to the screeching?" asked her quite astonished mom.

And her dad asked, "What about throwing yourself on the floor?"

Lulu replied, very dignified, "I'm one year older today, and I'm not doing that kid stuff anymore."

"And she says a very nice 'please,'" said the brontosaurus.

After the cake and the lemonade, the dinosaur said good-bye, but he would return for many holiday visits. Sometimes the snake and tiger and bear came too. Although she kept getting older, Lulu never turned into perfect. She still— though less and less often—sometimes screeched and forgot about "please," though she never again in her life said, "Foo on you." But she mainly wasn't a pain, and the brontosaurus was mainly not lonely anymore.

As for how all that stuff fit into Lulu's suitcase, I'm sorry to say that I don't have a clue. I am, after all, just the person who's writing this story.

The

End

LULU
Walks the Dogs

LULU
Walks the Dogs

JUDITH VIORST

illustrated by LANE SMITH

A Atheneum Books for Young Readers
atheneum

EW YORK • LONDON • TORONTO • SYDNEY • NEW DELHI

ATHENEUM BOOKS FOR YOUNG READERS
An imprint of Simon & Schuster Children's Publishing Division
1230 Avenue of the Americas, New York, New York 10020

This book is a work of fiction. Any references to historical events, real people, or real locales are used fictitiously. Other names, characters, places, and incidents are products of the author's imagination, and any resemblance to actual events or locales or persons, living or dead, is entirely coincidental.

For information about special discounts for bulk purchases, please contact Simon & Schuster Special Sales at 1-866-506-1949 or business@simonandschuster.com.

The Simon & Schuster Speakers Bureau can bring authors to your live event. For more information or to book an event, contact the Simon & Schuster Speakers Bureau at 1-866-248-3049 or visit our website at www.simonspeakers.com.

The text for this book is set in Officina Sans.

The illustrations for this book are rendered in pencil on pastel paper.

Library of Congress Cataloging-in-Publication Data
Viorst, Judith.
Lulu walks the dogs / Judith Viorst ; illustrated by Lane Smith. — 1st ed.
p. cm.
Summary: Lulu needs help from a boy named Fleischman if she is to earn money walking her neighbors' dogs, and she finds out that if she wants her business venture to succeed, she has to be nice.
ISBN 978-1-4424-3579-7 (hardcover)
ISBN 978-1-4424-3581-0 (eBook)
[1. Cooperativeness—Fiction. 2. Dogs—Dogs. 3. Dog walking—Fiction. 4. Moneymaking projects—Fiction.]
I. Smith, Lane, ill. II. Title.
PZ7.V816Luu 2010
[Fic]—dc23 2011023841

BOOK DESIGN BY MOLLY LEACH

For Daniel Luoh Hersh
—J. V.

For Strino and Creampuff
—L. S.

SINCE a kid named Fleischman
is going to hang around a whole lot
in these pages, I need to tell you
right away that Fleischman is not his
LAST name but his FIRST name.
Fleischman was his mom's last name
before she married his dad and
changed HER name to HIS, just
like other moms' last names could be

Got it? No? Well,
I'm busy, and it's time to

Anderson or Kelly before THEY got married. (Some moms don't change their last names after they're married, but I really don't feel like discussing that right now.) Anyway—stay with me here—some of these used-to-be Kelly moms might decide to first-name their daughters Kelly, and some Anderson moms might first-name their sons Anderson. Or maybe they'd name their sons Kelly and daughters Anderson. And though not too many Fleischman moms decide to name their kids Fleischman, Fleischman's mom did.

too bad if you don't.
tell my story.

chapter one

Lulu—remember Lulu?—used to always be a big pain, till she met Mr. B, a lovely brontosaurus. Now she is just a sometimes pain, and not nearly as rude as before. But unless what she wants is utterly, totally, absolutely, and no-way-José impossible, she's still a girl who wants what she wants when she wants it.

So, what is it, exactly, that our Lulu wants? Right now I'm just saying it costs a lot of money. Furthermore, her mom and her dad, who give her almost everything she asks for, said to her—with many sighs and sorries—that they couldn't afford to buy it for her and that she would HAVE TO EARN THE MONEY TO GET IT.

Lulu thought about throwing one of her famous screeching, heel-kicking, arm-waving tantrums, except that—since her last birthday—she wasn't doing that baby stuff anymore. So, instead, she tried some other ways—politer, quieter, sneakier, grown-upper ways—of changing their minds.

First try: "Why are you being so cruel to me, to your only child, to your dearest, darlingest Lulu?"

"We're not being cruel," her mom explained in an I'm-so-sorry voice. "You're still our dearest and darlingest. But we don't have the money to spend on things like that."

Second try: "I'll eat only one meal a day and also never go to the dentist, and then you can use all that money you saved to buy it for me."

"Dentists and food are much more important," Lulu's dad explained, "than this thing that you want. Which means"— and here he sighed heavily—"that if you really still want it, you're going to have to pay for it yourself."

Really still want it? Of course she really still wanted it! She was ALWAYS and FOREVER going to want it. But paying for it herself—that might be utterly and totally, plus absolutely and no-way-José, impossible. So she kept on trying to change their minds, making her saddest and maddest and baddest faces and giving her mom and her dad some unbeatable arguments. Like, "I'll move down into the basement, and you'll get the money by renting out my bedroom." Or, "You could get money by selling our car and taking the bus instead, which would also be much better for the environment." But, great as her arguments were, her mom and her dad kept saying no and sighing and sorrying. And after her sixteenth or seventeenth try, Lulu was starting to feel a little discouraged.

Last try: "So, while all the other kids are playing and laughing and having fun, I'll be the only kid my age earning money?"

"Oh, I don't know about that," said Lulu's mom. "That little Fleischman down the street is always earning money by doing helpful chores for folks in the neighborhood. So young and already such a hard-working boy!"

(Well, what do you know, here's Fleischman, and it's only Chapter One. I told you he would be hanging around a lot.)

chapter two

Lulu did not want to hear about hard-working Fleischman. She did not want to hear anything nice about Fleischman. She did not, in fact, want to hear anything about Fleischman. He was such a goody-goody, such a sweet little, kind little, helpful little boy, that Lulu could almost throw up when she heard him soppily say to the lady down at the corner, "You don't have to thank me, Mrs. King. It was an honor to hold your shopping bag." Or, "You paid me too much for raking your leaves, Mr. Rossi. Take back a dollar and keep it for yourself." Yecch! And when, in addition, the neighbors would say how cute, how adorable-looking Fleischman looked, Lulu would secretly wish that he would trip on his shoelace and knock out his front teeth.

Maybe you think that Lulu shouldn't be wishing such wicked wishes. Maybe you're right. But haven't you ever met someone who all the moms and the dads in the world thought was JUST PERFECT, someone you'd never be as perfect as, someone who, no matter what kind of excellent stuff you did, would always do more of it and do it better? (I knew a someone like that when I was a kid, and I still could almost throw up just thinking about her!)

But let's get back to the story.
Lulu needed to make some money.
And she didn't want Fleischman
getting in her way.

So she walked down the street to his
house, where he was sitting on his front
stoop playing his flute, which he did
whenever he wasn't earning money, or
getting the highest marks ever heard of
in school, or being completely adorable
by smiling his dear little smile and saying
to practically everyone he met, "Have a
great—I mean a really great—day." And
his shirt matched his pants, and his pants

matched his socks, and his hair didn't
have one single hair sticking up. Plus, next
to him was a bowl with a snack, and the
snack wasn't Sugar Clusters but sliced
carrots. Just looking at Fleischman made
Lulu so annoyed!

"Here's the deal, Fleischman," she
told him, with her hands on her hips
and her eyebrows scrunched together.
"I won't rake anyone's leaves or carry

their groceries. I won't mail a letter that someone forgot to mail. And in winter I won't help people pour salt on their sidewalks to keep them from slipping on the ice."

"That's interesting," said Fleischman, carefully putting down his flute and smiling his extremely annoying sweet smile. "But what's your point?"

"My point," said Lulu, not smiling back, "is that I'LL stay away from YOUR jobs. But I'm warning you, Fleischman, stay away from MINE."

"Which jobs are those?" asked
Fleischman, getting up from the stoop
and offering Lulu a carrot.

"As soon as I decide," she replied,
waving away the carrot, "I will
tell you."

Lulu went home and thought and
thought, and then she thought some
more, trying to figure out what her jobs
should be. But since the name of this
story I'm telling is *Lulu Walks the Dogs*,
you already know, of course, what
she decided.

chapter three

Well, maybe you already know and maybe you don't. Because maybe Lulu first decided her jobs—or job—should be baking cookies, or spying, or reading to old people, and then those jobs did not turn out too well. And maybe instead of writing a chapter about how those jobs did not turn out too well, I'm moving right along to Chapter Four.

chapter four

Lulu decided that if she got up earlier in the morning she could easily walk a dog before going to school. Somebody in the neighborhood must need a dog walker. Hey, maybe two different somebodies needed a dog walker. Hey, wait a minute, maybe even three. Lulu was certain that she could handle three. And if she charged two dollars and fifty cents a day per dog, and if she walked three dogs five days a week, in one week Lulu could earn . . . (Just give me a moment here—I'll tell you what she could earn. She could earn . . . Don't rush me! Okay—it's thirty-six dollars.)

(Excuse me, it is thirty-seven dollars and fifty cents. I've never been all that great at arithmetic.)

Using her mom's computer and printer, Lulu prepared an announcement that she stuck into all the mailboxes in her neighborhood. Here's what it said:

> LULU THE OUTSTANDING DOG WALKER
> WILL WALK YOUR DOG FOR $2.50 A DAY
> ON MONDAYS, TUESDAYS, WEDNESDAYS,
> THURSDAYS, AND FRIDAYS

Her announcement included her telephone number, so people could give her a call and make an appointment for her and the dog to meet.

By the end of Saturday afternoon, four neighbors had telephoned Lulu. One of these neighbors, however, was—guess who?—Fleischman. "You've got a dog to walk?" Lulu asked grumpily.

"I don't," Fleischman answered. "My mom's allergic to dogs. But I know all about them—I'm sort of kind of an expert. And after I read your announcement I thought that if you'd like, I could give you some advice."

That Fleischman had some nerve,
wanting to give her dog-advice when
he didn't even have a dog of his own!
Although, to be honest, Lulu didn't
either. "Thanks, but no thanks," said Lulu,
in a not-too-thankful voice. "What can be
so hard about walking a dog?"

chapter five

On Sunday, Lulu met three different dogs at three different houses, all in Lulu's neighborhood. Her mom went with her to every house, waiting outside on the sidewalk—just as she always did on Halloween—in case the people inside were witches or ogres. None of them were.

The first dog Lulu met was an enormous, bigheaded, bad-breathed brute named Brutus, who circled around her snarling and sniffing and sniffing and snarling and sniffing while Lulu waved her hand in a cautious hello.

"He's deciding whether he likes you," said Brutus's owner, who looked amazingly like Brutus. "We'll know that he does if he starts thumping his tail."

Lulu quit waving her hand and started saying, "Nice Brutus. Nice Brutus," though she didn't think that Brutus was nice at all. And after he had finally stopped with the circling and sniffing and snarling, and sat himself down in front of her, and glared at her out of his beady bright-red eyes, Lulu quit saying "Nice Brutus" and glared right back. And a little

while later, having decided they'd never
be New Best Friends, Lulu announced,
"Well, I'll be leaving now."

But as Lulu started to leave, Brutus
jumped up, ran over, and knocked her

flat down on the rug, then proceeded to lick her face and thump his tail. Brutus's owner pumped one fist in the air and announced approvingly, "He likes you. Brutus likes you. He really likes you. And

believe me, this is a dog that doesn't like everyone."

"And believe me," said Lulu, standing up and wiping globs of dog-slobber off her face, "I am a girl who also doesn't like everyone."

She was about to add that Brutus was among the everyones she didn't like when his owner said, "You're hired. You're hired. You're definitely hired. And furthermore, because Brutus is on the large side, I'm going to pay you fifty cents extra a day."

(On the LARGE side? Brutus was GIGANTIC—a mountain, a whale, an SUV of a dog!)

Still, two dollars and fifty cents and then another fifty cents made three whole dollars every single day, which meant that every five days Lulu would earn, well—after she figured out what she would earn, she decided that this was an offer she couldn't refuse. And so she nodded and said okay when Brutus's owner said to her, "See you Monday morning—six thirty sharp."

chapter six

_As_ Lulu walked down the street to her second appointment she started singing this money song, which all of a sudden had popped into her head:

Jimmy, Johnny,
Joseph, Jake.
How much money
will I make?
Laurie, Lucy,
Lynne, LaVerne.
How much money
will I earn?

Money! Money! Money! Money! Money!

By the time she had sung her song a few times she had come to the next house, where the doorbell was answered by someone who introduced herself to Lulu as Pookie's mommy. (She wasn't a dog, of course. She was a plump, pink human being with many curls. Did you really think that a dog had answered the doorbell, opened the door, and introduced herself?)

A teeny-tiny white fuzzball was nestled cozily against Pookie's mommy's chest and held in place by Pookie's mommy's left hand as Pookie's mommy explained (Hang in there, please—this sentence is *long*!) that though her little girl's name was spelled P-O-O-K-I-E, the POOK part rhymed with DUKE and not with BOOK, and that Pookie got very upset if she was called by a name that rhymed with the wrong word. "You'll never have a problem if you just remember DUKE," said Pookie's mommy—or PUKE, Lulu secretly thought but did not say. "Otherwise, you're sure to hurt her feelings, and trust me, you wouldn't want to hurt Pookie's feelings."

Lulu soon learned that the other thing that was sure to hurt Pookie's feelings was expecting Pookie to walk when Lulu walked her. "Here's how this works," Pookie's mommy explained. "*You're* the one who walks. Pookie gets carried. And when it's time, you'll sit her, gently, underneath a tree, and she will do what she's supposed to do."

"How will I know when it's time?" Lulu

asked. And Pookie's mommy answered, "Not to worry. She will let you know."

During this whole conversation Pookie never opened her eyes, not even when she was handed over to Lulu, who was urged by Pookie's mommy to practice saying Pookie's name several times.

"Nicely done," said Pookie's mommy to Lulu, after she'd finished practicing her OOKs. "I am offering you the job of Pookie's dog walker."

Lulu didn't think much of a dog that couldn't even be bothered to open her eyes. But she very much liked the twelve dollars and fifty cents that she would be paid every week to walk her. Remembering, as she did now and then, the manners she had learned from Mr. B, Lulu said to Pookie's mommy, "Thank you. I accept. I'll see you at six thirty-two on Monday morning."

chapter seven

The third house Lulu stopped at was a haunted-looking house, its yard overgrown with half-dead bushes and weeds, and all kinds of wrecked and rusted and ratty old furniture, pots, bikes, toys, and other junk piled helter-skelter on its sagging front porch. The skinny man and woman who answered the door in matching warm-up suits and baseball caps greeted Lulu warmly and then started poking around in the mess on the porch, with Mister explaining, "Our dog is in there somewhere," and Missus explaining, "Cordelia loves to hide."

Since Mister and Missus seemed to be having trouble finding Cordelia, Lulu joined in the hunt for the hidden dog, whose tail or ear or eye or leg would make a brief appearance, then once again vanish. Finally, Lulu, desperately trying to grab some part of Cordelia, instead knocked a broken-down bike off the top of the pile, which was followed by an avalanche of water-soaked books, chipped dishes, several window screens with holes, and . . . one yapping dog.

Lulu covered her head with her
hand to keep it from being bopped by
a falling screen. With the other hand
she reached out for Cordelia.

"Gotcha!" said Lulu.

"Good job!" said Mister and Missus,
who patted her shoulder and told her
she was hired.

And Lulu, handing them back their
dog, said to Mister and Missus, "I'll
see you Monday morning at
six thirty-four."

time-out

$\mathcal{I}$ can tell you already have questions for me, and I think I know what they are. So, why don't we take a time-out and get them over with?

Q: Shouldn't Lulu's mom and her dad stop her from trying to walk three dogs at once?

A: They should, but they won't. Lulu is hard to stop.

Q: What happened to Fleischman— didn't you say he'd be hanging around a lot?

A: I did, and he will be. Don't be in such a rush.

Q: How come Mister and Missus have all that junk piled up on their porch?

A: Beats me.
I've been wondering the exact same thing.

Q: What is it Lulu wants to buy with all this money she's earning?

A: I really don't feel like discussing that right now.

chapter eight

On Sunday night, before bedtime, Lulu carefully set the alarm clock for 6:25. She picked out the clothes she wanted to wear—so she wouldn't have to think about them in the morning. She tracked down her disappeared sneakers and carefully placed them next to her bed—so she wouldn't have to go looking for them in the morning. She even, to save a few seconds, squeezed some toothpaste onto her toothbrush—so she wouldn't have to squeeze toothpaste in the morning.

She figured that she could be dressed, washed, and tooth-brushed in three minutes and fifteen seconds on Monday morning, which would leave her forty-five seconds to eat some cold cereal, and one whole minute to run to Brutus's house.

Lulu was feeling extremely pleased with her plan. So, after saying good night to her mom and her dad and her pet goldfish and the photo of Mr. B that hung on her wall, she sang herself to sleep with a money song:

Danny, Donnie, Dustin, Dave.
How much money will I save?
Ava, Amy, Ann, Annette.
How much money will I get?
Money! Money! Money!
Money! Money!

Lulu expected to have some merry money dreams that night, but instead she dreamed all night about—guess who?— Fleischman. He was standing outside her front door and shaking his head and saying over and over again, "THREE dogs you're walking? Mistake. A big mistake."

chapter nine

Lulu woke up at 6:25, and for the first five minutes her plan worked perfectly. Dressed and washed and tooth-brushed in exactly, EXACTLY, three minutes and fifteen seconds? Check. Ate a bowl of cereal in precisely, PRECISELY, forty-five seconds? Check. Arrived at Brutus's house in one minute flat and rang the bell at 6:30 sharp? Check, and double-check, and for good measure check again. This girl was GOLDEN.

Brutus was happy to see her, so happy he knocked her flat down on the rug, slobbered all over her face, and thumped his tail. Brutus's owner was proud. "Is that cute or what?"

Lulu, who most definitely did not think it was cute, replied, "It's what." And then she stood up, wiped off, attached the leash to Brutus's collar, and—she was running a little bit late—was out the door, heading to Pookie's house.

I mean, she was TRYING to head to Pookie's house. Brutus was heading in a different direction. She pulled. He pulled.

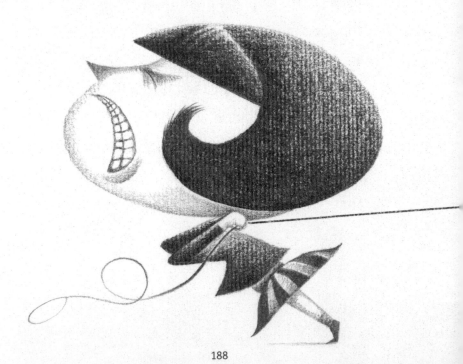

She pulled. He pulled. She pulled.
He pulled harder, making Lulu bang
into a tree.

Which gave her, along with a bump on
her knee, an idea.

Lulu began to wrap the long leash
around the trunk of the tree, wrapping it
so tightly around and around and around
the trunk that Brutus, two houses down,

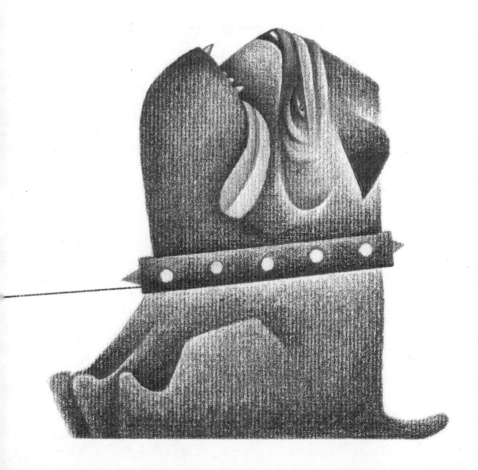

couldn't pull her anymore or go any
farther. Dog and girl had stopped moving,
and—across the space between them—
they were glaring at each other most
ferociously.

"We're doing it my way, Brutus," Lulu
announced in her bossiest voice.

"That won't happen," came the instant
reply. But in case you're thinking that
Brutus was speaking, you can think again.
The voice Lulu heard belonged—big
surprise!—to Fleischman.

Just the person she didn't want to see.

"You're just the person I didn't
want to see," said Lulu.

"Dog biscuits," Fleischman
mysteriously replied.

"Dog biscuits yourself," said Lulu, and went back to staring ferociously at Brutus: girl and dog still standing still—girl under a tree, holding on to one end of the leash, and dog, two houses down, attached to the other end—in a situation grown-ups call an impasse. (A complicated word that means neither one's going to do what the other one wants him to do.)

"If you're wanting Brutus to walk with you nicely to Pookie's house," said Fleischman, "you need a dog-biscuit trail for him to follow. And since I'm thinking you don't have any dog biscuits in your pockets, we'll use mine."

Fleischman walked over to Brutus and dropped a biscuit in front of his nose, which Brutus gladly and instantly gulped down. Then Fleischman turned around and walked back toward Lulu, dropping biscuit after biscuit on the ground, creating a tasty dog-biscuit trail that Brutus eagerly followed, gulping down biscuits. Soon thereafter, Fleischman and Brutus were standing next to Lulu under the tree.

"And now if you'll just unwind the leash from that tree trunk," Fleischman told Lulu, "we can get going."

Lulu, with Brutus on the leash and Fleischman walking ahead of them dropping biscuits, arrived without further fuss at Pookie's house. Lulu waited for Fleischman to leave. He didn't. Instead he said, "If you let me hold Brutus's leash while you go inside and pick up Pookie, we'll save some time."

"*We're* not saving time," said Lulu. "*I* am saving time. So wait out here with Brutus, if you want to, but I'm warning you, Fleischman, don't get any ideas."

"I'm not getting any ideas," said Fleischman. "I'm just happy to help. Happy and pleased and proud and delighted and honored and . . ."

"Quiet, Fleischman!" said Lulu in a voice that could shut up a city. "And stop being so happy."

chapter ten

Lulu was out of Pookie's house in twenty seconds flat, promising Pookie's mommy that she would be careful not to hurt the fuzzball's feelings. Holding Pookie with one of her hands and Brutus's leash with the other, Lulu was hurrying over to Cordelia's when Pookie—finally!—opened her eyes and wiggled. And then kind of squeaked. Then wiggled and squeaked some more. Lulu understood that this was Pookie's way of saying it was time to do what she was supposed to do. Which meant that Lulu needed to stop immediately and set down Pookie underneath a tree. Which she did and then said, in a not-too-patient voice, "Okay, let's get this over with. Do what you're supposed to do—right now."

"She won't if you talk like that," said
a voice that belonged—do I have to tell
you?—to Fleischman. "She needs to be
coaxed."

"I am not a person who coaxes," Lulu
told Fleischman. Then, bending down, she
repeated, "Pookie—right now!"

Except that when she spoke, instead
of the POOK part rhyming with DUKE,
Lulu forgot and rhymed it with—uh-oh!—
BOOK. Which turned out to be a mistake.
A big mistake.

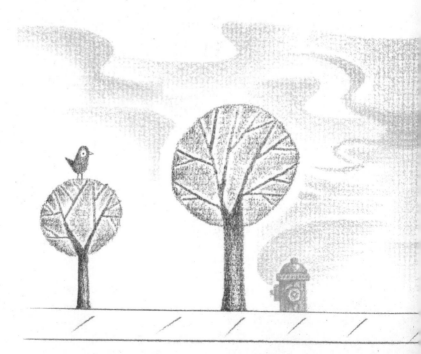

Pookie, yelping, leaped up in the air,
and instead of falling back down again,
she attached herself—by her teeth—to
Lulu's jean jacket. Lulu tried pulling her
off. Pookie hung on. Lulu tried pushing
her off. Pookie hung on. Lulu tried
shaking her off, but the once-lazy fuzzball
wouldn't let go, hanging on by her teeth
and somehow yelping at the same time,
which isn't that easy.

All of a sudden—out of the blue—
Lulu began to hear music. What was
this music? Where was it coming from?
Well—what do you know!—there was
Fleischman, who had taken his flute from
his backpack and was toot-toot-tootling
tunes into Pookie's ear.

"Fleischman!" yelled Lulu, still pulling
and pushing and trying to shake off
Pookie. "Cut out the concert!"

"This isn't a concert," said Fleischman. "This is coaxing."

Lulu watched with amazement as the yelping Pookie stopped yelping and hanging on by her teeth to Lulu's jacket. Instead, while Fleischman kept playing, Pookie let herself drop to the ground where, quietly squatting under the big leafy tree, she quickly did what she was supposed to do.

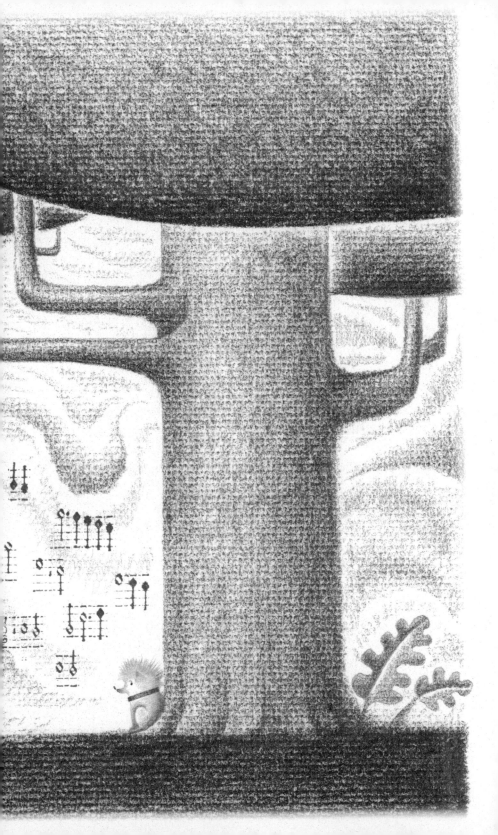

(Why is everyone saying that Pookie "did what she was supposed to do"? From now on I am going to just say "pooped.")

Fleischman whipped out a pooper-scooper, cleaned up the little mess, picked up Pookie, and handed her to Lulu. "Don't thank me," he told her, even though Lulu hadn't said a word. "Actually, I should be thanking you. I should be thanking you for letting me . . ."

"I don't want to hear it, Fleischman!" roared Lulu. "I really, really, really DON'T WANT TO HEAR IT. Now, out of my way, I'm seriously behind schedule."

time-out

$\mathcal{I}$ just this minute realized, even though I've already told you that Brutus is a great big, bad-breathed brute and that Pookie is a tiny, lazy, white fuzzball, I haven't yet said that—along with loving to hide—Cordelia is a long, low, short-legged, hot-dog-looking dog whose animal name starts with *d*, except I can't remember what comes after the *d*. Oh, and one more thing about Cordelia: She is very—and I mean VERY—vain.

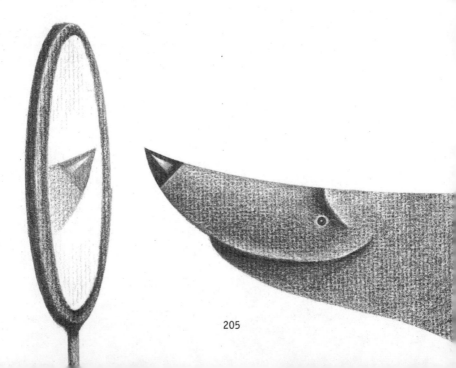

chapter eleven

Lulu, filled with impatience, was standing on Mister and Missus's porch—and she was late. Fleischman was waiting patiently under a tree. He was holding on to Pookie, who immediately fell asleep, and gently patting Brutus, who promptly pooped. Mister and Missus weren't upset about Lulu's being late, because they were busy looking for Cordelia. Who, even with Lulu's help, could not be found. Fleischman watched Mister and Missus and Lulu calling "Cordelia, Cordelia," as they poked and prodded the junk pile on the porch. And then, because it was getting too late and even though Lulu scowled a stay-out-of-this scowl, he joined them. Handing the two dogs to

Lulu, Fleischman knelt by the pile of junk and started speaking softly in a language that nobody else on that front porch knew. Well, nobody but Cordelia, because as soon as he started talking, she came popping out of the pile and, yapping blissfully, went waddling over to Fleischman.

"It's Cordelia!" shouted Mister.

"It's Cordelia!" shouted Missus.

"It's time," Lulu announced, "for me to go." Quickly taking over, she attached Cordelia's leash to Cordelia's collar, and holding on to all three dogs—Pookie against her chest, the others on leashes— she turned to Fleischman, nodded, and said, "I'm leaving."

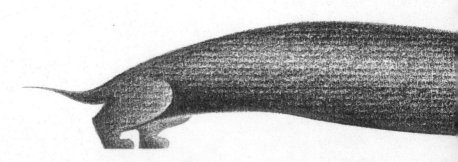

(That nod was maybe Lulu saying thank you. Or maybe not.)

Fleischman, though not invited, was leaving with Lulu. But Mister and Missus first had two questions to ask. What kind of language did Fleischman speak to Cordelia? And what exactly did he say to her?

"I spoke in German," Fleischman explained, "because Cordelia's a dachshund, and dachshunds are German. I also know how to talk to French poodles in French." Then he told Mister and Missus what he said to Cordelia to make her come out of hiding, but I really don't feel like discussing that right now.

chapter twelve

$\mathcal{Six}$ and a half minutes later, evening up with Brutus and Pookie, Cordelia pooped.

chapter thirteen

Lulu needed to get back home, or else she'd be late for school. But she also needed to bring the dogs back to their owners. "I can do that," said Fleischman. "I don't have school today. They're giving me the day off because I'm so smart."

Lulu knew she should thank him, but she really, really, really wanted to stomp him. Wouldn't you?

Still, as Fleischman went off with Cordelia and Pookie and Brutus, and Lulu pulled up her socks and hurried home, she forgot about all the difficulties of the morning and thought about all the money she'd already earned. Which inspired her to sing a money song.

Howie, Harry, Harvey, Hank.
Lots of money for my bank.
Goldie, Gracie, Gladys, Glor.
Lots of money for my drawer.

Money!

Money!

Money!

Money!

Money!

(Lulu thinks it's okay to use the name "Glor" to rhyme with "drawer" because, she says, Glor is a nickname for Gloria. I'm not so sure.)

After school on Monday, Lulu remembered all the difficulties of the morning and decided she'd have to SPEND some money to make some. She went to the market and bought the cheapest dog

biscuits she could find. She went to the toy store and bought, for only sixty-nine cents plus tax, a plastic toy flute. And

then she went to the library and took out, from the language section, an easy-looking book called *Beginner's German*.

She figured it wouldn't take much to learn what she needed to learn to make the dogs behave. She figured that she would do just fine without Fleischman.

chapter fourteen

She didn't. Brutus hated the taste of Lulu's cheap dog biscuits. Pookie yelped when Lulu toot-toot-tootled the toy plastic flute in her ear. And Cordelia, who either did not understand or pretended to not understand Lulu's German, kept right on hiding. In other words, Tuesday was just as bad as Monday. Fleischman, who was hanging around, asked Lulu if he could help her. Lulu sighed and said a grouchy, "Okay."

chapter fifteen

Lulu bought better dog biscuits, practiced harder on the flute, and memorized saying in German (though it made her want to throw up), "You are the bestest, most beautiful dog in the world." But Wednesday was worse than Monday and Tuesday combined because Brutus wouldn't start walking, and Pookie wouldn't stop yelping, and Cordelia hid so well that she couldn't be found, in addition to which Brutus missed and pooped all over Lulu's foot—maybe on purpose. Fleischman, who was hanging around, asked if he could help. Lulu sighed and said a grouchy, "Okay."

chapter sixteen

$\mathcal{O}n$ Thursday, after a morning
TWICE as bad as Monday and Tuesday
and Wednesday combined, Lulu told
Fleischman she'd hire him as her
assistant. She said she would pay him
thirteen dollars a week.

chapter seventeen

Thirteen dollars a week—is that fair? Let me figure this out. Lulu is getting twelve dollars and fifty cents a week for Cordelia, and another twelve dollars and fifty cents for Pookie, and a great big fifteen dollars a week for Brutus. Add all these up and she gets, every week . . . she gets, every single week . . . she gets, every single week—I'm close, I'm close, I'm almost there—she gets, every single week, forty whole dollars!

And she wants to give Fleischman,
who works just as hard, maybe harder, a
measly thirteen dollars every week? That
doesn't seem one bit fair to me but—hold
it!—listen to what Fleischman is saying.

"I don't want your money, Lulu. I am
happy, delighted, thrilled to help you for

free. It's truly my pleasure to serve you, to . . ."

"Fleischman, stop it right now!" Lulu roared. "Or I'm throwing up, right now, on your perfect sneakers."

Fleischman shrugged his shoulders and stopped it right now.

chapter eighteen

On Friday and for the next two weeks,
Lulu—along with Fleischman—walked the
dogs. They each took turns making dog-
biscuit trails for Brutus. They each took
turns coaxing Pookie by tooting the flute.
And they each took turns saying the most
flattering things in German to Cordelia to
persuade her to come out of her hiding
place. And as long as Fleischman was
there, the dogs behaved.

Lulu didn't have much to say to
Fleischman. She didn't want Fleischman
saying much to her. But on their third
Friday together, after the dogs were
returned to their owners, Fleischman
tapped Lulu's elbow and said to her
quietly, "We make a good team."

Big mistake.

Lulu stopped walking and started
scowling at Fleischman. She put her
hands on her hips. She narrowed her eyes.
"Fleischman," she said to Fleischman, "I

want you to listen, and listen carefully. We aren't a team. We will NEVER be a team. I'm the dog-walking boss, and you are only my assistant. *¿Comprendez?*"

(*Comprendez* is Spanish for "Do you understand?" But why, you may very well ask, did she say it in Spanish? I really don't feel like discussing that right now.)

Fleischman nodded his head to show that yes, he understood. And then he turned and silently headed home.

chapter nineteen

Patrick, Preston, Paulie, Pete.
Money for my special treat.
Julie, Jackie, Jenny, Joan.
Money for myself alone.
Money! Money! Money!
Money! Money!

Lulu sang a money song as she hurried to Brutus's house on Monday morning. Fleischman was usually waiting for her outside. Except today there wasn't any Fleischman. Lulu gave him a minute. And then she gave him two minutes. And then she gave him three minutes—

"Three strikes and you're out," Lulu said to no one in particular. After which she announced, "So what if Fleischman isn't here. I'm going to walk these dogs all by myself. I know I can walk these dogs all by myself." She took a deep breath and said out loud, sounding a lot more sure than maybe she was, "I'M READY TO WALK THESE DOGS ALL BY MYSELF."

And I have to admit that, for a little while, Lulu actually looked as if she were ready.

Because:

Brutus followed obediently as Lulu dropped biscuits and made him a dog-biscuit trail.

Pookie listened politely as Lulu coaxingly tooted her flute, after which she (as in Pookie, not Lulu) pooped.

And Cordelia, after Lulu said some gooey blah-blah-blahs to her in German, was persuaded to waddle out of her hiding place.

But as soon as Mister and Missus waved good-bye to their Cordelia and closed the front door, the morning got worse than it ever had been before.

Lulu, standing under a tree, said to the dogs, in one of her bossiest voices, "Okay, let's move it—Brutus! Cordelia! Pookie!"—except she forgot, and rhymed the POOK part with BOOK. (This, as you may remember, hurts Pookie's feelings. Which, as you may remember, you don't want to do.)

Pookie, leaping up high in the air, fastened her pointy teeth onto Lulu's jean jacket, holding on tight and yelping at the same time, while Cordelia slipped out of her collar and went dashing back onto the porch, where she hid herself deep, deep down in the pile of junk. As all this was going on, big Brutus, who wasn't as dumb as he looked, circled wildly around and around the tree trunk, wrapping his leash around it just as tightly as Lulu had done on their very first walk together. And Lulu, who had been leaning against the tree as she tried (and kept failing) to shake off Pookie, discovered—too late! too late!—that she had been totally tied, by Brutus's leash, to the trunk!

Totally, utterly, absolutely, embarrassingly, humiliatingly tied.

She couldn't move her arms. She couldn't move her legs. She couldn't chase after Cordelia or shake off Pookie. And she certainly couldn't untangle herself from the leash, still attached at the other end to Brutus, who was standing just out of her reach, triumphantly woofing.

(And if you find it hard to believe when I tell you that Brutus tied up Lulu on purpose, remember who's in charge of this story—me!)

Lulu wriggled and wriggled, but she couldn't get herself loose. So, after a while, she stopped wriggling and began to think about what she could do to get loose. And after a longer while, she started wriggling some more. Until finally, after feeling that she had been tied forever to the trunk of that tree, Lulu saw—well, you know who she saw— Fleischman.

Yup, there he was, good old Fleischman,
strolling slowly down the street, playing
"You Are My Sunshine" on his flute.

Just the person Lulu did not want
to see.

Just the person Lulu needed to see.

Just in time to take another time-out.

time-out

$\mathcal{I}$ think we ought to discuss what's going on here.

I don't feel one bit sorry for Lulu— do you? You remember I said back in Chapter One that, since she met Mr. B, Lulu wasn't as big a pain as she'd been. And not nearly as rude. But she sure was being extremely rude to Fleischman. Rude! Rude! Rude! And also ungrateful! For Fleischman helped her over and over, and said he was happy to help, and didn't even want money from her for helping. And all Lulu did was boss him around and threaten that she would throw up on him, plus she wouldn't be his friend, or even his teammate. Maybe she needs to keep staying tied to that tree until she says, "I'm sorry, Fleischman."

Wait, I think she just whispered, "I'm sorry, Fleischman."

chapter twenty

Well, it turns out that Lulu didn't exactly say, "I'm sorry, Fleischman." What she actually said to him was, "Untie me, Fleischman," followed ten or twenty seconds later by a growly sounding "please."

Fleischman stopped tooting and stood right in front of the very grumpy, very tied-up Lulu. "*Teammates* untie each other," Fleischman told her. "But I'm not your teammate."

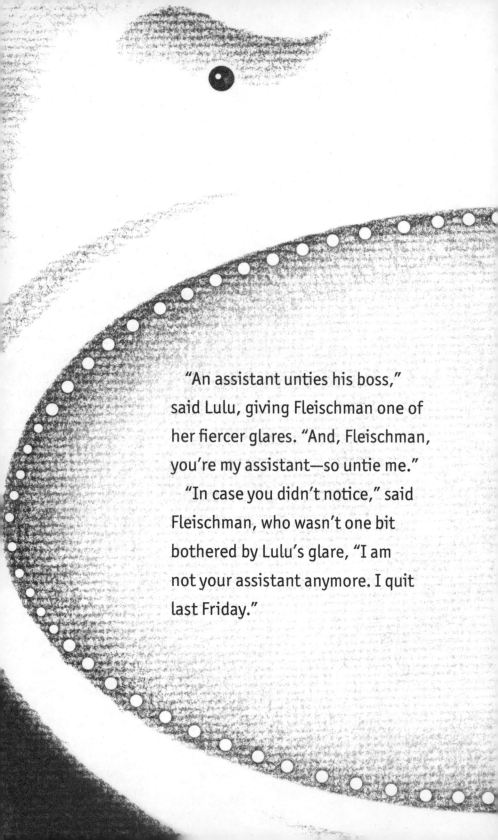

"An assistant unties his boss," said Lulu, giving Fleischman one of her fiercer glares. "And, Fleischman, you're my assistant—so untie me."

"In case you didn't notice," said Fleischman, who wasn't one bit bothered by Lulu's glare, "I am not your assistant anymore. I quit last Friday."

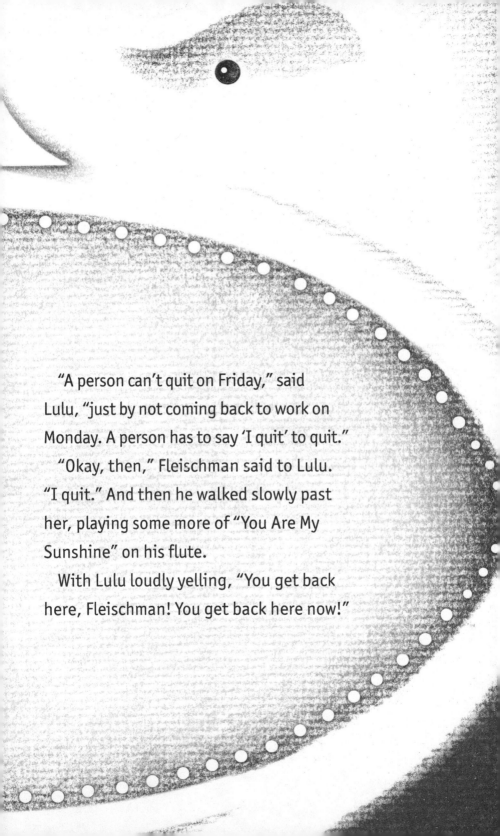

"A person can't quit on Friday," said
Lulu, "just by not coming back to work on
Monday. A person has to say 'I quit' to quit."

"Okay, then," Fleischman said to Lulu.
"I quit." And then he walked slowly past
her, playing some more of "You Are My
Sunshine" on his flute.

With Lulu loudly yelling, "You get back
here, Fleischman! You get back here now!"

time-out

$\mathcal{I}$ think that I need to mention that, by this time, Lulu and Fleischman were quite late for school. But although, for several hours, they weren't where they should have been, not one single person noticed they weren't there. Not Lulu's teacher. Not Fleischman's teacher. Not any of their classmates. No one!

Plus, nobody walking down that street—and lots of people were—seemed to notice that Lulu was tied to a tree. And not just tied to a tree, but wriggling and yelling and making quite a remarkable fuss. (In actual life this almost never could happen. In the stories I write, things like this happen a lot. Deal with it.)

Oh, and I think I should mention that, by this time, Pookie had fallen sound asleep, let go of Lulu's jacket, and dropped to the grass, where she curled in a tight white fuzzball and yawned a great big yawn and kept on sleeping. And that Cordelia, bored with hiding under the junk pile—with nobody trying to find her, it wasn't much fun—waddled over to Pookie, flopped down right beside her, and soon

was snoring very loudly, in German. And
that Brutus, his heavy head drooping
lower and lower, was just as deep asleep
as the rest of them. Except for Lulu, of
course, who was wide awake and still
screaming, "Get back here, Fleischman!
Now!"

chapter twenty-one

Fleischman got back there.

"Okay, I'll untie you," Fleischman said to Lulu. "But only if you'll explain how come you hate me."

"Oh, I can do that," said Lulu. "That'll be easy." And then she gave him ten different explanations:

"You're always eating carrots.

"You never eat anything that's bad for you.

"Your sneakers look like they just came out of a store.

"You play an actual flute instead of a toy one.

"You wear that ugly T-shirt that says,

(I didn't mention this earlier because that T-shirt makes *me* want to throw up.)

"You have this really, really annoying smile.

"You keep saying things like you can speak German and French.

"You keep saying things like 'I'm honored and thrilled to serve you.'

"You got a day off from school because you're so smart.

"You're a total expert on dogs—and you don't even *have* a dog.

"All the moms and the dads in the world think you're perfect, and maybe you are, and how can a person not hate a person who's perfect?

(Okay, so I made a mistake. Lulu gave him *eleven* explanations. But forget about that—right now I am anxious to hear what Fleischman will say. Aren't you?)

chapter twenty-two

Except, for a while, Fleischman didn't say anything. He was busy untying Lulu from the tree, which turned out to be much harder than he, or she, or even I had ever expected. Before he was finished, however, he took a deep breath and said to Lulu, "It's not fair to hate a person because he's perfect." And then he added, so softly she barely could hear him, "Besides—I'm not perfect. I am *so* not perfect."

So not perfect? Fleischman was *so* not perfect? Hmmm.

"Keep talking, Fleischman," Lulu said to Fleischman, looking pleased for the very first time that day. "Stop trying to untie me, and tell me more." Fleischman stopped untying and told her more.

"I don't change my underpants every single day.

"You wouldn't believe the mess that's under my bed.

"I'm scared of the dark.

"I'm also scared—make that

ABSOLUTELY TERRIFIED—of crawly-creatures like caterpillars and worms.

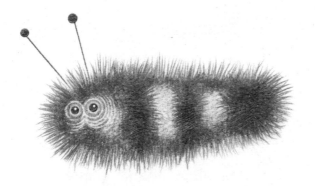

"I can only speak German to dachshunds and French to poodles. Whenever I try to speak German or French to humans they can never understand me.

"I play the flute because I already tried and couldn't play the violin, the piano, the guitar, the clarinet, the drums, and the *gusli*." (The what? The WHAT? I really don't feel like discussing that right now.)

Lulu kept listening cheerfully until Fleischman was done telling more and went back to untying. And then she—looking even more cheerful—said, "Terrified of crawly creatures! Smelly underwear! Can't play the *gusli*!"

Fleischman shrugged. Lulu kept on talking. "But what about all that goody-goody stuff—the carrots, the sneakers, the smile? Plus being so honored and thrilled? Plus being so smart?"

"That's who I am," said Fleischman. "I can't help it. Just like you can't help"—and all of a sudden he started to speak in a very loud voice—"that you are really, really dumb about dogs. Plus, you certainly aren't the nicest girl in the world."

(Whoa! Listen to Fleischman! Who ever knew that he could talk that way!)

Lulu glared at Fleischman. Fleischman glared at Lulu. But instead of an impasse, they had a conversation—a quite noisy conversation that lasted the rest of the morning and all of the afternoon. There was yelling (from Lulu) and crying (from Fleischman) and yelling (from Fleischman) and crying (from Lulu) and (from both of them) much stamping of feet. But when they were finished with all of that, Lulu and Fleischman shook each other's hand.

chapter twenty-three

From that day on, Lulu and Fleischman were more than boss and assistant and more than teammates. They were, in fact, partners, with Lulu offering Fleischman (and making him take) exactly half of the money she earned walking dogs, and promising to teach him (for only ten dollars) how not to be scared of caterpillars and worms, plus whispering (in a voice he hardly could hear, but at least she said it) that although she had no wish to be the nicest girl in the world—boring! too boring!—she would try her very best to be nicer to him.

(Somewhere deep in his forest,
Mr. B is slowly nodding his head
and smiling.)

Fleischman, in return, promised that
he'd give away the shirt that says I'M
HERE TO BRING SOME HAPPINESS INTO YOUR
LIFE, teach her (for only ten dollars) to
understand dogs, try his very best to
stop saying how honored and thrilled
and delighted and smart he was, and
work on smiling a less annoying smile.

Did Lulu stop hating Fleischman? Yes,
she did. Did Lulu stop being rude to
him? Yes, she did. Was Lulu now willing
to talk with him while they walked the
dogs together on weekday mornings?
Yes, she was. And so, did Fleischman
and Lulu finally turn into New Best
Friends? No, they did not.

You want a happy ending? Read *Cinderella*. This story has only sort of a happy ending. Because Fleischman is still too annoying for Lulu to love. And Lulu is still too fierce for Fleischman to love. They respect each other. They count on each other. They're partners and dog-walking buddies. If one of them got tied up, the other would help. But unless they turn into totally different people, I'm pretty sure they won't be New Best Friends.

Still, the last time I saw them together they were walking Brutus and Pookie and Cordelia. Lulu was trying to kick some dirt on Fleischman's perfect sneakers. Fleischman was shaking a carrot in Lulu's face. And as they got near the end of the street I could hear them loudly singing this money song:

Larry, Liam, Lester, Lou.
All this money for us two.
Cathy, Carly, Chloe, Claire.

All this money we can share.
Money! Money! Money!
Money! Money!

the last time-out

I'm sure you have some more questions for me, and I think I know what they are. So I guess I should try to help you find the answers.

Q: How come some moms (like Fleischman's mom) change their last name when they marry, and some moms don't?

A: Different moms are going to have different reasons, so go ask your own mom why she didn't or did. And how come, if she changed her last name, she didn't give you a first name like Anderson, or Kelly, or even Fleischman.

Q: Why in the world did Lulu say, "*¿Comprendez?*," rather than saying, "Do you understand?"

A: She was hoping that Fleischman would think that she was able to speak Spanish. She actually can't.

Q: What did Fleischman say the first
time he talked to Cordelia in German?

A: He told her she had won first prize in the International Dachshund Beauty Contest. She actually hadn't.

Q: Is there a musical instrument called the *gusli*?

A: There is. But only a Fleischman would want to play it.

Q: So what is this superspecial thing that Lulu wants to buy, this thing that she says she will want FOREVER and ALWAYS, this thing that her mom and her dad keep saying (with many sorries and sighs) they cannot afford, this expensive and wonderful thing that Lulu will someday be able to pay for with the money she has earned by walking the dogs?

A: I really don't feel like discussing that right now, but if you insist, I guess we'll have to go into overtime.

overtime

Q: *Okay,* so now we're in overtime, and I'm asking you once more: What is this superspecial thing that Lulu is going to buy when she earns enough money?

A: What Lulu is hoping to buy, what Lulu is planning to buy, what Lulu is GOING to buy is . . . a seat on a spaceship. She wants to be the very first kid in all the entire world to take a journey into outer space.

Q: That's impossible, right?

A: Impossible? What do you mean, impossible? Have you forgotten who is writing this story?

Q: But wouldn't a seat on a spaceship cost at least a million dollars?

A: No, a seat on a spaceship would cost at least TWENTY-FIVE million dollars. But Lulu convinced the people in charge to take away some zeros so she'll only have to pay twenty-five hundred dollars.

Q: But if Lulu makes forty dollars a week, and she's giving half to Fleischman, won't it take her forever to earn enough money?

A: Not really. Lulu says that it's going to take two years and twenty-one weeks of walking the dogs. Which definitely is worth it, she says, to be the very first kid in outer space.

Q: The first kid in outer space: Won't that be lonely?

A: Actually, no. Lulu says that as long as he absolutely understands that he'll just be the SECOND kid in outer space, she is going to save a seat for Fleischman.

The

End

LULU'S
Mysterious Mission

LULU'S

Mysterious Mission

JUDITH VIORST

illustrated by KEVIN CORNELL
cover by LANE SMITH

Atheneum Books for Young Readers

EW YORK • LONDON • TORONTO • SYDNEY • NEW DELHI

ATHENEUM BOOKS FOR YOUNG READERS
An imprint of Simon & Schuster Children's Publishing Division
1230 Avenue of the Americas, New York, New York 10020

ATHENEUM BOOKS FOR YOUNG READERS is a registered trademark of Simon & Schuster, Inc.

Atheneum logo is a trademark of Simon & Schuster, Inc.

For information about special discounts for bulk purchases, please contact Simon & Schuster
Special Sales at 1-866-506-1949 or business@simonandschuster.com.

The Simon & Schuster Speakers Bureau can bring authors to your live event.
For more information or to book an event, contact the Simon & Schuster Speakers Bureau
at 1-866-248-3049 or visit our website at www.simonspeakers.com.

The text for this book is set in Officina Sans.

The illustrations for this book are rendered in graphite and watercolor on paper and then digitally manipulated.

Library of Congress Cataloging-in-Publication Data
Viorst, Judith.
Lulu's mysterious mission / Judith Viorst ; illustrated by Kevin Cornell ; jacket by Lane Smith. — 1st ed.
p.   cm.
Summary: When Lulu's parents go on vacation, the formidable Ms. Sonia Sofia Solinsky comes to babysit and
Lulu behaves as badly as possible to get her to leave until Ms. Solinsky reveals her secret.
ISBN 978-1-4424-9746-7
ISBN 978-1-4424-9748-1 (eBook)
[1. Babysitters—Fiction. 2. Behavior—Fiction. 3. Spies—Fiction.] I. Cornell, Kevin, ill. II. Smith, Lane. III. Title.
PZ7.V816Lvm 2014
[Fic]—dc23   2013004350

To the Viorst grandsons:
Nathaniel, Benjamin, Isaac, Toby, and Bryce
—J. V.

For Kim, who holds my hand
—K. C.

STOP! *Don't begin the*

I need to tell you. And I think I'd better

This isn't a book about Lulu's Mysterious Mission. It's actually about Lulu's Babysitter. And that's what I wanted to call it except two kids that I know, Benjamin and Nathaniel, kept telling me that *Lulu's Babysitter* was a really boring title. Which means that the name of this book has absolutely nothing at all to do with the story I'm writing.

You have now been warned!

Wait! Now that I have warned you, I am feeling a tiny bit guilty.

first chapter just yet. There's something *tell it to you* right now.

Like maybe it isn't fair to trick readers like that. Like maybe there ought to be a law that what's INSIDE a book has to somehow match up with the NAME of the book. So maybe—I'm not *promising*, but just maybe—I'll put in some stuff about a Mysterious Mission.

Meanwhile, either return this book or keep reading. You'll find out what happens when Lulu meets up with Ms. Sonia Sofia Solinsky, who is definitely not your Mary Poppins–type babysitter.

And you *might* find out about a Mysterious Mission.

chapter one

But first let's go find Lulu, who isin the living room screeching "No! No! No!" although she doesn't screech much anymore. However, the news she was hearing from her mom and her dad was so utterly, totally SHOCKING that it not only started her screeching but almost shocked her into throwing one of her heel-kicking, arm-waving, on-the-floor tantrums. Lulu, however, thinks of herself

as too grown-up now to throw tantrums.
Which also means she thinks of herself as
grown-up enough to go with her mom and
her dad on the trip they just told her that
they would be taking WITHOUT HER.

When Lulu had finished screeching, she
fiercely glared at her mom and her dad
and asked them—in a not-too-nice voice—
these questions:

"How can you have a good time if I'm
not there?"

And "Who's going to take care of me,
and how can you be positive that this
person won't kidnap me and hold me
for ransom?"

And "Or maybe she'll stop feeding me and start yelling at me and hitting me and locking me down in the basement with the rats." (Okay, that isn't technically a question.)

When Lulu was done, her mom and her dad looked at each other, then answered—very carefully. For even though their daughter wasn't the serious pain in the butt that she used to be, she wasn't the easiest girl in the world to be parents to when she didn't get her way.

"First of all," said Lulu's dad, "there are no rats in our basement. As a matter of fact, we don't even HAVE a basement."

"But even if we did," said Lulu's mom, "we'd never hire a sitter who'd lock you up in it. Or starve you or hit you or yell at you or kidnap you."

"Or," added Lulu's dad, "hold you for ransom."

"And if you were held for ransom," Lulu's mom assured Lulu, patting her oh-so-lovingly on the cheek, "we'd pay whatever it took to get you back."

"But," Lulu pointed out, removing her mom's patting hand from her cheek, "if instead of paying the ransom, you'd let me come with you, this trip of yours would cost a lot less money."

Lulu's dad explained that as much as they loved and adored their precious only child, they wanted to have—for the first time since they'd been parents—a private grown-ups-only vacation together. And that even though they wouldn't be having the kind of fun they had with their fabulous Lulu, they would be having a DIFFERENT kind of fun.

"You mean BETTER fun," grumped Lulu. "You'll have better fun without me. And you won't even care when I get sick and die."

chapter two

Lulu's mom started crying at the thought of poor little Lulu, left behind and dead of a broken heart. "Maybe . . . ," she sniffled to Lulu's dad, "maybe we ought to stay home. Or take her with us. Maybe we are being too unkind."

It's at this point in every argument that Lulu almost always gets her way because her mom and her dad just cannot BEAR it when their darling is displeased. It's right at this point that Lulu almost always gets what she wants because her mom and her dad give up and give in. Except on those rare occasions—like now, for instance—when they try NOT to.

Lulu's dad cleared his throat, and in a strong, firm voice replied to Lulu's mom. "No," he said. "We're going. She's staying. THAT'S what we decided and"—he took a deep breath—"we're sticking to it."

He then turned to Lulu and said, "But you don't have a thing to worry about, dearest darling. Because, after much research, we've hired the best babysitter in town—maybe the world—to take care of you the week that we're away."

"Babysitter?" Lulu gasped. "Babysitter? Babysitters sit babies, and I'm no baby."

(Lulu thinks she's no baby because she plays a tough game of Scrabble, goes by herself to the corner store to buy milk, gets good reports from her teachers, earns some money walking dogs, rides a bike with no hands, and has pierced ears. She's also on the softball team, the swim team, and the debate team; has recently started learning the trombone; and is going to be a crossing guard next year. And what Lulu wants to know is why a person who can do all that would need a person called a *baby*sitter.)

"Call her what you want, but her name," Lulu's mom said soothingly, "is Ms. Sonia Sofia Solinsky, a trained professional. And we're sure, dear, that if you, dear, will give her, dear, a chance, dear, the two of you will get along just fine."

"In fact," said Lulu's dad, "she's moving in this afternoon. We'll show her around the house, and maybe you two can start to bond before your mom and I leave tomorrow morning."

(Tomorrow morning? They're leaving tomorrow morning? How come Lulu is only now being told that her mom and her dad are leaving tomorrow morning?

How come she wasn't told earlier? How come she wasn't given time to prepare? As the person who's writing this story, I take full responsibility for this decision. Because anyone who knows Lulu like I know Lulu wouldn't want to give her time to prepare.)

"I'm going up to my room," said Lulu to her mom and her dad. "And maybe I'll come down and maybe I won't. But while I'm up there," she added as she loudly tromped up the stairs, "I'm planning to be very very unhappy."

chapter three

Up in her room, along with being very very unhappy, Lulu was trying to figure out what to do. Actually, she knew WHAT to do: get rid of the babysitter so her mom and her dad would have no one to leave her with. All she needed to figure out was HOW.

She went to her computer—yes, she has her own computer; she has her own *everything*—and typed in "How To Get Rid of a Babysitter." But nothing too helpful came up, so Lulu started making a list of possibilities, and as she wrote she chanted this little chant:

Eeny meeny miney mo,
That babysitter's got to go.

While Lulu was chanting and making her list, the doorbell rang and a voice boomed through the house, a voice that sounded to Lulu like real bad news. "Sonia Sofia Solinsky," it said. "At your service."

Lulu heard the gentle murmurs of her mom and her dad, interspersed with Ms. Solinsky's boom, and the quiet patter of their feet, interspersed with Ms. Solinsky's clomp, and then someone (either her mom or her dad) was knocking softly at her bedroom door, with Ms. Solinsky bellowing, "The eagle has landed, Lulu. Open up."

("The eagle has landed"? That's how Ms. Solinsky says hello?)

Lulu, thinking fast, took off her shoes, jumped into bed, and huddled pitifully underneath her comforter, hoping to make all three of them believe that she had suddenly been struck down with some

dreadful disease. And so, when she heard her mom calling, "Come out, my darling, and meet Ms. Solinsky," she said, "I think that I just got real sick."

"Probably not," said Lulu's dad. "You looked perfectly fine to me only an hour ago."

"But I'm not fine now," Lulu replied. "I think I'm very sick. And, anyway, I'm definitely contagious."

"Not a problem," Ms. Solinsky boomingly replied. "I never catch anything."

She then—the nerve!—turned the doorknob, opened Lulu's bedroom door, and marched herself straight over to Lulu's bed.

chapter four

The sight of Ms. Solinsky, with her long unsmiling face and her hair yanked back in a tight little, mean little bun, was not the kind to gladden a young girl's heart. She was dressed in some sort of uniform that a General of All Generals might wear, with binoculars and a metal

canteen hanging down from the belt that held up her pants, and a jacket bedecked with several silver medals, along with rows of badges and ribbons and stars. On her feet were heavy, thick-soled, high-top, lace-up combat boots, the kind that could stomp almost anything into dust. And over her shoulder she hauled a bulging duffel bag, stuffed from bottom to top with who knows what. Anyone else, after taking one look at Sonia Sofia Solinsky, would have shivered and shuddered and instantly said, "I surrender."

(Maybe you're starting to wonder why Lulu's mom and Lulu's dad would ever hire someone who would wear a menacing uniform and combat boots. All I can tell you is, first, everyone said that Ms. Solinsky was the best babysitter in town—maybe the world—and, second, she may not have looked like that when they interviewed her.)

But she sure looked like that now, and, as I already pointed out, anyone else would have shivered and said, "I surrender."

Not Lulu.

Indeed, when Ms. Solinsky reached her hand out for a handshake, Lulu, instead of politely reaching back, crossed her arms across her chest and tucked her hands emphatically into her armpits. "Maybe you can't catch something from me, but I," said Lulu, "might catch something from you. And maybe what I might catch could make me even sicker than I already am."

"Well, aren't you the sensible one!" Ms. Solinsky exclaimed. "But still—no problem." She dug into her duffel bag, pulled out a packet of disinfectant wipes, and briskly wiped down her hands—first left, then right. "I've just killed off my germs, which means you can't catch

something from me," she said to Lulu. "So now"—she reached out again—"shall we shake hands?"

Although there was a question mark at the end of this last sentence, this wasn't a question.

Lulu shook hands.

After the handshake Ms. Solinsky told Lulu's mom and her dad that if they wanted to pack for their trip, she would stay with Lulu and keep her company. "We'll do just fine," she assured them as they gratefully rushed from the room, moving so fast that they didn't see Lulu frantically shaking her head and

mouthing (so Ms. Solinsky wouldn't hear
her), "Don't go."

The minute they were gone Ms. Solinsky
brought her unsmiling face down close to
Lulu's and said, "That I'm-so-sick routine
may work out great in a storybook or in
a movie, but don't waste my time trying
it on me. You're in excellent health, and
I want you on your feet, in your shoes,
standing tall, arms straight down at
your sides in exactly"—she looked at her
wristwatch—"ninety seconds."

No grown-up in Lulu's entire life had
ever dared to talk to her that way. And
no grown-up, Lulu decided, would be

allowed to. And so, without saying a word, she pulled the comforter over her head and pressed her body hard into the mattress. She could hear Ms. Solinsky counting down—"eighty seconds . . . sixty seconds . . . thirty-five . . . twenty-five . . . fifteen seconds . . . time's up." And then, without taking a breath, Ms. Solinsky swooped an astonished Lulu out of her bed, set her onto her feet and into her shoes, pushed back her shoulders, lifted her chin, and pressed a firm palm against her droopy spine.

And—what do you know!—there was Lulu, standing tall, head high, her arms straight down at her sides. Looking good. But not quite good enough.

"Hmm," muttered Ms. Solinsky as she walked around her, carefully checking her out, "I see we have a lot of work to do."

chapter five

From that time on, until Lulu's mom and her dad went away the next morning, Lulu had not one moment just with them. Whenever they knocked at the bedroom door, Ms. Solinsky bellowed, "We're still bonding," though, in fact, what they mostly were doing was glaring. At dinner Ms. Solinsky was right at Lulu's side. And early on Saturday morning, when Lulu's mom and her dad were kissing her good-bye and Lulu was getting ready to make-believe faint in one last effort to stop them from going, Ms. Solinsky was stationed directly behind her, holding tight to the back of her skirt so she couldn't fall.

As her mom and her dad headed out to the taxi, Lulu heard her mom saying, "If things don't work out with Lulu . . ."

And her dad saying, ". . . and it's just possible that they won't . . ."

And her mom saying, ". . . call us, and we'll take the next plane home."

To which Ms. Solinsky firmly replied, "When I'm the babysitter, things ALWAYS work out."

"We'll see about that," Lulu said to herself, preparing for Plan B, which was doing whatever she had to do to get her parents to take the next plane home.

Then the door slammed, and Lulu was all alone with Ms. Solinsky, trained professional.

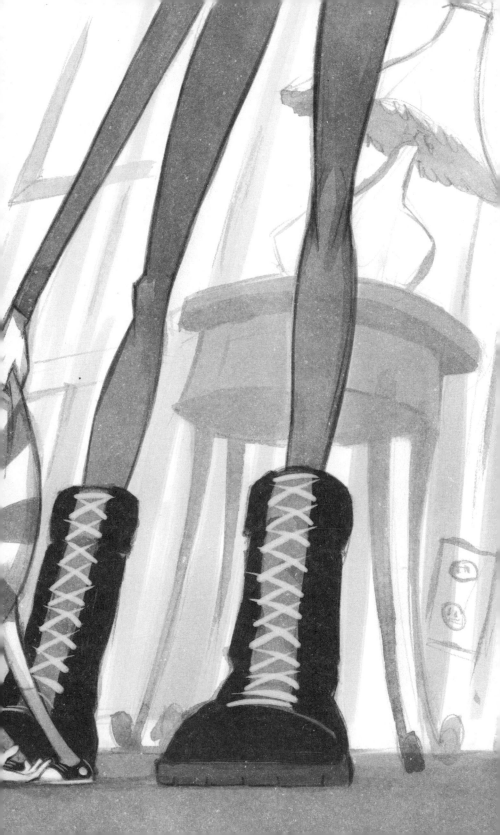

chapter six

Ms. Solinsky smiled at Lulu with the kind of smile that an alligator might give you just before that alligator ate you for dinner. It was not the kind of smile that made the person being smiled at want to smile back. It was more the kind of smile that gave you a headache, a stomachache, and a lump in your throat.

"Maybe I really AM sick," Lulu told her.

"Could be," said Ms. Solinsky. "But lucky for you, I've got just the cure. A nice brisk run around the block—three times. It will put some fresh air into your lungs and some pink into your cheeks.

And it will give you a great appetite for the bean-and-beet omelet I'm making for your breakfast."

(Lulu—you won't be surprised to hear—doesn't do brisk runs or bean-and-beet omelets. The last time she had a brisk run was when she was briskly running away from Mr. B, a delightful brontosaurus who, after a little misunderstanding, became her best friend. And a bean-and-beet omelet sounded like something her dog-walking-partner and sort-of-friend Fleischman would eat because, although utterly disgusting, it was so good for him.)

Now those of us who know Lulu would have expected her to screech, "Brisk run? Bean-and-beet omelet? You must be kidding me!" But screeching wasn't part of Lulu's Plan B. Instead, she said, in a fake sweet voice, "I'll just go upstairs, Ms. Solinsky, and get my sneakers."

"And be quick about it," answered Ms. Solinsky.

"Yes, sir," said Lulu, clicking her heels and saluting at the same time.

"I am not amused," said Ms. Solinsky.

As Lulu headed up the stairs, she cheerfully, though softly, chanted this chant:

Eeny meeny miney mo,
That babysitter's got to go.
Hot or cold or sun or snow,

chapter seven

When Lulu reached the second floor she didn't go to her bedroom to get her sneakers. That hadn't ever been a part of her plan. Instead, she went to the bathroom, opened the window, and climbed out onto the tree that grew there. A tree she had very often climbed onto and down from—right down into her backyard.

Her plan, when she reached the ground, was to find a hiding place in the neighborhood while Ms. Solinsky waited for her inside, waited and waited until she finally went upstairs and found that open window. After which Lulu intended to keep on hiding while Ms. Solinsky kept on searching for her. After which Lulu intended to still keep hiding while Ms. Solinsky—trained professional though she might very well be—would have to call Lulu's mom and her dad to say, "I've lost your daughter. You need to get on the next plane and come home."

As to what, exactly, they'd do to the babysitter who had lost their precious daughter, Lulu was quite certain that they would get rid of her, hopefully having first stripped her of every one of her medals and ribbons and badges and stars. As to what, exactly, Lulu planned to tell her mom and her dad about why she had hidden from the babysitter, Lulu was quite certain that between now and then she would figure something out.

"Eeny meeny miney mo," Lulu chanted again as she slid down the tree trunk. "That babysitter's got to go," she chanted as her two feet hit the ground. "Hot or cold or sun or snow," she continued, pulling her socks up and tucking her shirt in. But before she could finish another "That babysitter's got to go," a loud "ahem!" disturbed her happy mood.

Standing at strict attention at the bottom of the tree—and what, in heaven's name, was she doing out there?—was none other than Ms. Sonia Sofia Solinsky.

"What, in heaven's name, are you doing out here?" Lulu fake-sweetly asked her. "I was just getting ready to meet you by the front door."

"I very much doubt that," said Ms. Solinsky, scowling down at Lulu and shaking a stern finger in her face. "But

I'm warning you, don't bother trying that climb-out-the-window-and-down-the-tree nonsense again. Believe me, I know tricks that you've never dreamed of. Besides which, you were already wearing your sneakers."

She then grabbed Lulu's hand and said, "It's time for our brisk run. And forget what you're thinking—I'm not letting go."

chapter eight

Three laps around the block later, Lulu was back in her own kitchen eating a hideous, horrible bean-and-beet omelet. She was also still plotting how to get rid of Ms. Sonia Sofia Solinsky, who wasn't sounding that easy to get rid of.

"It's almost time for my trombone

lesson," Lulu told Ms. Solinsky. "It's just a few blocks away. I can go by myself."

"You won't be going anywhere by yourself," said Ms. Solinsky. "I promised your folks I'd watch over you, and I will. And since this morning's escapade, I will be watching over you very carefully." She then explained what "very carefully" meant:

"It means that I will be going with you to your trombone lesson today and to the front door of your school to drop you off and pick you up every day next week, as well as to the bathroom every night when you take a bath, as well as to your dog-walking job on Monday, Tuesday, Wednesday, Thursday, and Friday. Any questions?"

"Yes, sir," said Lulu. "Will you also be going along with me when I throw up your delicious bean-and-beet omelet?"

"I am not amused," said Ms. Solinsky.

"Me either," Lulu said to her, heading out the door with her trombone and—of course!—Ms. Solinsky. And shortly thereafter the two of them were standing outside the house of—I'll explain this to you in a second—Harry Potter.

chapter nine

So let me explain.

Harry Potter, to everyone's bemusement and confusement, is Lulu's trombone teacher's actual name, which forces him to have to reply, whenever he meets someone new, "Sorry. No. *Not* Harry Potter, boy wizard. The *other* Harry Potter, trombone teacher." He also, much too often, has to put up with all kinds of incredibly stupid jokes about spells and potions and wands and flying broomsticks. It makes me kind of wonder, since I am the person writing this story, if maybe I should have found him a different name. But though I'm the first to admit that this might have saved him a lot of trouble, sometimes a writer has to make tough choices.

By this time, Harry Potter had opened
his door and invited Lulu and Ms. Solinsky
to come inside and have a seat in the
living room. "There's something I need
to take care of," he told them, "so make
yourselves at home. I'll be ready for you in
just a couple of minutes."

Ms. Solinsky—her posture perfect;
her mouth in a stern, straight line—sat
down at one end of Harry Potter's couch.

Lulu—chin on the palms of her hands,
and elbows on her knees—sat far down on
the other end of the couch. A clock ticked
loudly in the unfriendly silence.

All of a sudden, Ms. Solinsky leaped
up off the couch. She was coughing and
sneezing and gasping and wheezing! And
coughing and sneezing and gasping and
wheezing! Then coughing and sneezing
and gasping and wheezing some more!

"Cats! There must be cats in this house!" she said in a croaky voice, rubbing her now bright-pink and watery eyes. And just as she spoke, Harry Potter returned, saying apologetically, "Sorry to keep you waiting, but I really had to feed my hungry cats."

"To which," Ms. Solinsky announced, dabbing a handkerchief to her eyes, "I'm sorry to say I am seriously allergic."

"But," Lulu asked, displaying (I'm sorry to say) a most unfortunate absence of sympathy, "weren't you bragging just yesterday that—and I'm quoting directly—'I never catch *anything*?'"

"An allergy," Ms. Solinsky said in the iciest of voices, "is something that you *have*, not something you *catch*." She then explained that in order to keep her allergy from getting much, much worse, she would need to wait for Lulu outside the house.

"But RIGHT outside the house," she told Harry Potter. "Ready to take charge of her the instant that her trombone lesson is done."

"We'll see who's taking charge here," Lulu said—but just to herself. And then, but just to herself, she chanted:

Eeny meeny miney mo,
That babysitter's got to go.

Hot or cold or sun or snow,
That babysitter's

Soon, not later; fast, not slow,
That baby

got to go.

sitter's got to go.

And then, but just to herself, she
said, "And now I know what to do to
get her going!"

chapter ten

Lulu made a lot of mistakes during her trombone lesson because her brain was busy with her new plan. And as soon as her lesson was done and she was back upstairs in her room, she sent out messages by e-mail and cell phone.

All the messages said the same thing.

All of them were sent to Lulu's friend Mabel.

Do you remember Mabel? Of course you don't. Neither do I. But I am about to. And right now the most important thing that all of us need to remember about Mabel is that she is the owner of two cats. Because Mabel plus Two Cats equals Plan C.

Which is why each of Lulu's messages

was marked top secret and said: "Bring your cats to my house right now for a sleepover," though some of them said it like this: "Top ckret—brng ur katz 2 my hse rite now 4 a sleepovr."

While Lulu waited for Mabel she chanted her chant and, in between verses, pondered three questions.

Eeny meeny miney mo,
That babysitter's got to go.

 Q: How long would it take two cats that had been secretly stashed in Ms. Solinsky's bedroom to make her start coughing and sneezing and gasping and wheezing?

Hot or cold or sun or snow,
That babysitter's got to go.

 Q: How long would it take for her allergy to go from serious to much, much worse?

Soon, not later; fast, not slow,
  That babysitter's got to go.

Q: And how long before she had to telephone Lulu's mom and her dad to say, "Cats! I can't live with cats! Your daughter's attacking me with cats! You need to get on the next plane and come home"?

Up and down and to and fro,
  That babysitter's got to go.

Less than ten minutes after Lulu had
sent out her urgent messages, she looked
out her bedroom window and there was
Mabel. She was pumping sturdily down
the street and balancing in the basket of
her bike something craftily covered up by
a blanket. That covered-up something,
Lulu was sure, was the carrier people use

when they take a pet on a plane or to a sleepover.

Mabel was a girl who could be counted on to understand "top secret."

Lulu rushed down the stairs and was heading out the front door to meet Mabel when she heard a voice roaring somewhere overhead, "Halt! Stop! Cease and desist! Don't move! Hold it right there!"

Lulu halted.

But then the voice continued, "Listen up, Mabel. This means you. Halt or you will be under arrest for trespassing."

Lulu ran outside and looked around for Ms. Solinsky, whose voice (as all of us know, of course) it was. But the sitter was nowhere in sight until another "Cease

and desist" made Lulu look upward. And
there, her combat boots firmly planted on
the roof of the house and her loud voice
made louder by a megaphone, was Sonia
Sofia Solinsky, her medals gleaming in the
afternoon sun.

And there, just beyond Lulu's driveway,
was the usually super-cool Mabel, off her
bike and stuttering, "But . . . but . . . but . . .
but . . ."

"Time to leave now," said Ms. Solinsky

to an astounded Mabel. "Trespassing is a criminal offense."

"Mabel isn't trespassing. I invited her. She's visiting me," said Lulu. "What is your problem?"

"No problem," said Ms. Solinsky, "because I know from your top secret messages that Mabel has been invited to come with her cats. And since I'm severely allergic to cats, she and they will have to leave. Immediately."

Mabel, cool girl though she was, was feeling alarmed at the possibility of maybe going to prison for criminal trespassing. "Sorry, Lulu!" she shouted, and then, accompanied by meowing sounds from her basket, she jumped on her bike and swiftly pedaled away.

When Ms. Solinsky came down from the roof, Lulu indignantly asked her, "How did you know that Mabel was bringing cats? How did you know what I wrote in my top secret messages? How did you ever find out what I was doing in the privacy of my own bedroom?"

"I have my ways," Ms. Solinsky replied. "I am a trained professional. Which is why I'm hired by parents all over town—maybe the world—to babysit their especially difficult children."

Lulu, more indignant than ever, glared at Ms. Solinsky. "Are you telling me that my mom and my dad think that I'm an especially difficult—"

"I'm not," Ms. Solinsky broke in, "telling you anything. I'm merely pointing out that, thanks to my training, I'm able to know when a person is not really sick, or is planning to climb out a window and go into hiding, or is writing top secret messages, which—thanks to my training—I'm able to read immediately."

Lulu moved on from indignant to outraged. "Isn't it rude," she demanded, "to read messages that haven't been sent to you?"

"Not as rude as bringing in cats when a person's allergic to cats," replied Ms. Solinsky.

After which the two of them had nothing whatsoever to say till Lulu's bedtime.

chapter eleven

You might imagine that Lulu, getting ready to go to bed, was feeling discouraged. Wrong! Lulu is not a girl who discourages easily, in spite of the fact that her sick plan, her hide plan, her bring-in-the cats-plan—all of them!—had failed. No, Lulu was not discouraged. She was . . . thinking.

She was thinking that she had just finished spending a whole, entire, totally bossed-around Saturday in the company of Sonia Sofia Solinsky. And THAT WAS ENOUGH. THAT WAS MORE THAN ENOUGH! She promised herself that by the end of Sunday, she was absolutely, positively, utterly, no doubt about it getting this babysitter out of her life.

Lulu lay in bed thinking, and chanting her chant:

Eeny meeny miney mo,
That babysitter's got to go.

Hot or cold or sun or snow,
That babysitter's got to go.

Soon, not later; fast, not slow,
That babysitter's got to go.

Up and down and to and fro,
That babysitter's got to go.

Forehead, belly, knee, and toe,
That babysitter's got to go.

Lulu tossed and turned in her bed—
thinking, chanting, thinking, chanting—
and then she smiled a wide and wicked
smile. She had another plan (and yes, I
know that it's her fourth plan, Plan D),
but this was the one she was certain
was going to work. For tomorrow
Lulu intended to teach Ms. Sonia
Sofia Solinsky the true meaning of an
especially difficult child.

chapter twelve

On Sunday morning Ms. Solinsky awakened Lulu early, telling her to get ready for another brisk run and another bean-and-beet omelet. Lulu leaped out of bed and rushed around the room to get ready, but NOT for another brisk run and horrid omelet.

The first thing she did—and this took enormous effort—was to push her dresser against her bedroom door, wedging it under the doorknob to make it hard, almost impossible, for Ms. Sonia Sofia Solinsky to come in.

Next she turned on her stereo and
television set, raising the volume as
loudly as it would go, and joining in,
just as loudly, with some truly terrible
tunes on her trombone. (Lulu wasn't
all that great at playing the trombone;
she made it sound like a hippo with a
stomachache—but I'd rather you didn't

tell her that I said so.) She finally, very carefully, put earplugs in her ears, and waited for the pounding at the door.

It didn't take long at all for Ms. Solinsky to be pounding at the door.

"Turn off that noise," she commanded, "and open up—now!"

But although she spoke and pounded so loudly that Lulu could hear her in spite of the noise and the earplugs, Lulu sweetly answered, "Sorry, can't hear you."

Ms. Solinsky kept pounding and pushing at Lulu's bedroom door, demanding, "Turn off that noise and open up!"

Lulu kept sweetly repeating, "Sorry, can't hear you."

Then Ms. Solinsky used both of her fists to pound against the door, yelling, "Turn off that noise and open up!"

Once again Lulu replied, "Sorry, can't hear you."

Then Ms. Solinsky raised one of her

feet (remember those heavy
combat boots?) and aimed
a mighty kick at Lulu's
door, roaring as she kicked
(and roaring's much louder
than either commanding,
demanding, or yelling),
"TURN OFF THAT NOISE AND
OPEN UP RIGHT NOW!"

And Lulu, just as sweetly as
before, once again replied,
"Sorry, can't hear you."

Next came a long and what
some might call a terrifying
pause. Then Ms. Solinsky
bellowed (which is even
louder than roaring), "DON'T
YOU DARE SAY SORRY TO ME.
I KNOW THAT YOU CAN HEAR

ME. SO NOW HEAR THIS: I AM COMING IN!"

The next thing Lulu heard was Ms. Solinsky running to the end of the hall and then running back—full speed— toward her bedroom door. And the next thing Lulu saw was Ms. Solinsky crashing through that heavy door and

knocking down the dresser blocking the door. Once past all these obstacles, she turned off Lulu's loud stereo and TV, after which she put her combat boots to use again by stomping Lulu's trombone into dust.

There were broken bits of door and dresser all over Lulu's bedroom. A lampshade was crushed; a chair was minus

one arm; the trombone was ruined, of course; and some green gooey glop, which used to be Lulu's science experiment, had dribbled out of its jar and now was stickily, stinkily splattered on the rug. Lulu studied the mess in her room and smiled a very big, very satisfied smile. Because, strange as it may seem to you, things were going exactly as she had planned.

chapter twelve
and
one half

As you've probably already noticed, we're more than halfway through this story, and I still haven't mentioned Lulu's Mysterious Mission. But before you start complaining, kindly keep in mind that I warned you that I might not. On the other hand, I also said that maybe—just maybe—I might, and I still might. So calm down.

chapter thirteen

As Lulu and Ms. Solinsky stared at each other across the wreckage of the room, Lulu began to chant her little chant:

Eeny meeny
miney mo,
That babysitter's
got to go.

Hot or cold
or sun or snow,
That babysitter's
got to go.

Soon, not later; fast,
not slow,
That babysitter's
got to go.

Up and down
and to and fro,
That babysitter's
got to go.

Forehead, belly,
knee, and toe,
That babysitter's
got to go.

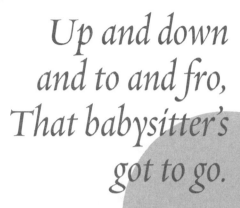

Ha-ha-ha
and ho-ho-ho,
That babysitter's
GOT TO GO.

This time, however, Lulu didn't bother
to chant her chant secretly—under
her breath, to herself, or alone in her
bed. Instead, she chanted it loudly and
outrageously
and shamelessly,
while standing
face to face with Ms. Solinsky.

Who was not amused.

"You are," she told Lulu, "an impudent,
insolent, insubordinate child! Impossible!
Incorrigible! Insufferable!"

"I'm not quite sure what all those words mean," said Lulu to Ms. Solinsky. "Why don't you give me a minute to look them up?"

"I am not amused," said Ms. Solinsky.

"But *you* are in trouble," said Lulu. "In really big trouble. I'm taking pictures"—and that's what (*click, click, click*) she started doing—"of how you completely and totally wrecked my room. And"—(*click, click, click*)—"I'm ready to send them, right this minute, to my mom and my dad."

"And why would you do that?" asked Ms. Solinsky.

"Because when they see what you've done to my room," said Lulu, "I'm sure they'll be flying back home on the very next plane."

(Well, what do you know?! Just as you maybe suspected! This was Lulu's Plan D, and it has worked!)

"I did what had to be done," Ms. Solinsky told Lulu. "I make no apologies. That's what it means to be a trained professional."

"But that's probably not what it means to be," Lulu said, "and I'm quoting directly, 'the best babysitter in town— maybe the world.'"

"Let me say once again that I make no apologies," Ms. Solinsky told Lulu. "But clearly my training to be a babysitter wasn't nearly as exhaustive or effective as my training to be a spy."

WHOA! WHOA! WHOA! WHOA! WHAT WAS *THAT*? *WHAT* IN THE WORLD WAS *THAT*? *WHAT* DID MS. SOLINSKY JUST SAY?

"Excuse me," gasped an astonished, astounded, amazed, and goggle-eyed Lulu. "Did you just say 'spy'?"

"I did," Ms. Solinsky reluctantly replied. "I never should have said it—that was a terrible breach of security—but I did."

"You personally were trained to be a spy?" asked a stupefied Lulu.

"Trained and served as a spy," said Ms. Solinsky loudly and proudly—she was

clearly enjoying Lulu's adoring attention. "Code name Triple S."

(Another security breach—but never mind.)

CODE NAME? SHE HAD A CODE NAME? TRIPLE S WAS HER CODE NAME? LULU *LOVED IT.*

"So wait," Lulu said. "You trained and served as a spy and now you're . . ."

"A former spy. A retired spy. And, at present, a full-time babysitter whose specialty, you may recall, is babysitting especially difficult children."

The especially-difficult-children stuff should have made Lulu angry all over again. Except she was way too thrilled about the spy stuff.

She stood there, saying nothing, but

her brain was churning, churning. After which it churned and churned some more. After which came the following conversation:

Lulu: "A former spy. A retired spy. Not a spy anymore. But it sounds like you still remember how to do it."

Ms. Solinsky: "Of course I remember. Once a spy, always a spy."

Lulu: "And did you—may I call you Triple S?—did you, Triple S, have lots and lots of amazing spy adventures?"

Ms. Solinsky: "Amazing AND successful. In fact, I was so good at my work that I wound up being named Head of All Spy Training."

A spy so good that she was a trainer of spies! Lulu was so excited she hardly could breathe. She pressed a hand against her chest to calm her pounding heart and then asked the question that she was burning to ask.

"Would you, could you, please, dear Triple S"—did she just say *dear*?—"would you stay here and train me to be a spy?"

Train her to be a spy? Lulu wanted spy training from the very exact same woman about whom she'd repeatedly been chanting those most exceptionally unfriendly chants?

Ms. Solinsky looked long and coldly at Lulu. "Excuse me," she said, "but what's happened to all those cute little eeny meeny miney mos? What's happened to those photographs you were sending to your parents to get them to fly back home on the very next plane? Weren't you only recently trying all kinds of fiendish tricks to get me to go? And now, all of a sudden, you want me to *stay*?"

Lulu hung her head. She was actually embarrassed. But Lulu being Lulu, she only stayed embarrassed for a few seconds.

"It's true," she told Ms. Solinsky, "that I wanted you—the babysitter—to go. But I definitely want you—the spy—to stay. I just this minute decided that I want to be a spy when I grow up. And you are the perfect person to teach me how."

"Why would I want to do that?" asked Ms. Solinsky.

"Because I really want you to," answered Lulu.

"That's IT?" said Ms. Solinsky. "Because you WANT me to? Do you usually get what you want just because you WANT it?"

"Usually," said Lulu. "Are you saying yes?"

"There's no reason in the world for me to say yes," said Ms. Solinsky.

"Actually, there is," said Lulu, a warning tone in her voice. "If I send out these

pictures of my wrecked room to my mom
and my dad, plus the entire universe,
everyone will think that you're the WORST
babysitter in town, maybe the world.
Sonia Sofia Solinsky, trained professional?
Hah! Your reputation would be . . . dog
poop!"

"You are without a doubt," said Ms.
Solinsky, "the most especially difficult of
all the especially difficult children I've
babysat."

"But I wouldn't be," said Lulu, suddenly switching to a pretty-please tone of voice, "if I were being trained as a spy instead of being babysat by you. I'd obey your every command. I'd do whatever you told me to. I'd WANT to do brisk runs and bean-and-beet omelets."

Ms. Solinsky, whose face had been as stern and as stony as something carved on a mountain, seemed to be softening—just a little bit. She did not want Lulu's parents to come home and

fire her. She did not want her reputation to be dog poop. And training a spy would certainly be more interesting than being a babysitter, even if the spy she'd be training was Lulu.

"TOTAL obedience?" she asked.

"Total," Lulu promised.

"I'll get back to you with my answer in an hour," said Ms. Solinsky. "Meanwhile, clean up as much of this mess as you can."

Lulu started to say no way was she

cleaning up this mess, and then she
realized that wasn't a good idea. Instead,
she stood up straight, clicked her heels,
saluted, and said, "Yes, sir," to Ms.
Solinsky. Except this time, she was saying
it so earnestly, so respectfully, so politely
that Ms. Solinsky wasn't not amused.

chapter fourteen

$\mathcal{D}uring$ the hour that Lulu worked on her room and waited for Ms. Solinsky's answer, she started chanting a new, friendlier chant:

G F E D C B A,
Triple S has got to stay.
June or April, March or May,
Triple S has got to stay.

"She's GOT to stay and train me!" Lulu kept saying to herself in between chants. "I really really really really really want to learn to be a spy."

Sixty minutes later, Ms. Solinsky, now toting her duffel bag, was standing once again in Lulu's bedroom. Looking around, she could see that though the room remained really wrecked, Lulu had tried hard to put it back together.

"I've considered your request," Ms. Solinsky told Lulu, "and I am prepared to offer a qualified yes. By 'qualified' I mean, first, you can't discuss the training with anybody. Ever. And second, if you challenge even one of my instructions, I will give up teaching you spy craft— at once!—and return—at once!—to babysitting you. Get it?"

Lulu was thrilled beyond thrilled. "I get it! Just give me my instructions. I want to learn *everything*!"

Today was still Sunday (in case you

forgot) and Lulu's parents were coming home Friday night, so Ms. Solinsky had only six days to train Lulu. And Lulu, of course, would also need time for her school and homework and trombone and dog-walking job, plus all her other busy, busy activities. But while Ms. Solinsky warned Lulu that becoming a full-fledged spy took *years* of training, "I'll have time to teach you a set of important basics."

Beginning, she announced, with Repair and Restore, which was also known as R and R.

Ms. Solinsky explained that spies, using special spy keys and other implements, can open any locked door they wish to open. However, she said, they may sometimes (like today) encounter certain obstacles (like a dresser) that require

them to *crash* through a door instead.
Spies also, said Ms. Solinsky, can leave
any room that they have entered and
searched (and wrecked) looking exactly
as it had looked before, so that no one
would ever know that they had been
there. And that was why one of a spy's
basic skills was Repair (fix whatever
needs fixing) and Restore (make it look
as if it never happened).

"And that," Ms. Solinsky told Lulu, "is
what you now are going to do with your
wrecked bedroom."

"Ridiculous! Impossible!" said Lulu,
sounding like the old Lulu again.

"There's a great big hole in my door and my dresser drawers are all smashed up, and my trombone is dust, and my chair . . ."

"Do 'impossible' and 'ridiculous' mean you're refusing to obey?" Ms. Solinsky asked warningly.

"Of course that's what it . . . ," Lulu began, then—catching herself—continued, "DOESN'T mean. 'Impossible'? 'Ridiculous'? Not with Triple S as my spy teacher!"

"That is correct," Ms. Solinsky said, "and now"—she reached into her duffel bag—"let's get started."

Out of her bag came a jar of extra-strength rug wash, a large tube of superglue, and a vacuum cleaner designed to retrieve and reverse. (I'll explain about that in just a couple of seconds.) Barking out instructions, Ms. Solinsky guided Lulu as she glued all the broken pieces smoothly together and scrubbed

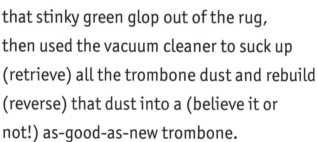

that stinky green glop out of the rug, then used the vacuum cleaner to suck up (retrieve) all the trombone dust and rebuild (reverse) that dust into a (believe it or not!) as-good-as-new trombone.

When the work (most of which Lulu had done) was finished, and the furniture had been pushed back into place, no one would ever have guessed that it had been otherwise. No cracks where the breaks had been mended! No stain where the rug had been scrubbed! And when Lulu tested her rebuilt trombone, it (and she) sounded better than before!

"You have made a promising start," Ms. Solinsky told Lulu, who smiled a proud smile. "And now I need to see you destroy those pictures you took of the room in its wrecked condition. I can't take the slightest chance of having my reputation besmirched," which is a fancy way of saying "turned to dog poop."

Lulu kind of liked the idea of keeping those wrecked-room photographs in case she ran into problems with Ms. Solinsky. On the other hand she knew that there was only one thing she should do and that was . . . obey.

chapter fifteen

On Monday afternoon, after school, Lulu rushed into her house, yelling, "I'm home, Ms. Solinsky, and ready for training."

(Some clever readers will wonder why Ms. Solinsky wasn't waiting outside Lulu's school. Some even cleverer readers will figure out that it's because Ms. Solinsky is now Lulu's spy trainer—not her babysitter.)

There was no answer. Lulu yelled a few more times, then ran upstairs and checked out all the rooms, repeatedly calling Ms. Solinsky's name. Still no answer.

Back downstairs again, Lulu went racing
from room to room, her heart beating
fast as she called out, "Ms. Solinsky!" But
the house was empty—at least it seemed
empty—until Lulu reached the kitchen,
where she saw someone sitting quietly on
a chair. That someone definitely wasn't
Ms. Solinsky.

What Lulu saw instead was a stranger—a
woman as beautiful as a movie star—with
long blond hair and big blue eyes and a
slinky blue dress that perfectly matched

her eyes. And though, as we all know, our Lulu is not the kind of girl who frightens easily, she was shocked and alarmed to encounter this awesome blonde.

"*Who* are you?" Lulu demanded. "And *why* are you here? And *what* have you done with Ms. Sonia Sofia Solinsky?"

The beautiful stranger smiled at Lulu, tossed her long blond hair, and then replied in a voice as sweet as candy. "But, Lulu," she said to her, "I AM Ms. Solinsky."

Lulu was fainting. Well, not really fainting, but feeling so weak and wobbly in the knees that she had to sit herself down before she fell down. (And actually, though I'm the one writing this story, I also am feeling just a little faint.)

"I don't understand. I'm so confused."
Lulu was almost babbling. "How can
you be you when you have turned into a
totally different person?"

Ms. Solinsky corrected her. "I have
turned MYSELF into a different person.
We're finished with R and R, and now
we're moving on to basic spy lesson two,
which is known as D and P—Disguise and
Penetrate."

Ms. Solinsky explained that an
extremely important spy-craft technique
was the ability to Disguise your
appearance so totally that even those
closest to you wouldn't know you were
you. Just as important, she added, was
being able to Penetrate, see through,

others' disguises, so you'd always be able to tell that they were them.

"We'll work on D and P today and tomorrow," Ms. Solinsky said to Lulu, who—completely recovered from her shock—said, "Great! Let's go!"

Ms. Solinsky explained that she had spent all Monday morning searching through her duffel bag for various items to transform Lulu into—

"Into who?" asked Lulu, exploding with curiosity. "Who will I be?"

"You'll see in due time," Ms. Solinsky said. "We'll do them one by one, and after each

transformation you'll look in the mirror.
But remember, I want no complaining and
no argument."

No complaining? No argument? This was
asking a lot—maybe too much—of Lulu.

Still, looking in the mirror after
being disguised as a boy, Lulu had no
complaints—she liked what she saw. With
her hair tucked into a baseball cap, a sleek
black leather jacket, and some fake brown
freckles sprinkled across
her nose, she'd been
handsomely transformed
from Lulu to Lou.

She was also okay—not thrilled, but okay—with the sight of herself disguised as a middle-aged woman, with glossy makeup, a raincoat, and high heels, though she certainly could have done without the ugly orange purse and the frizzy hair.

It was only when the mirror reflected—
to Lulu's absolute horror—a pudgy,
pigtailed three-year-old girl in pink
sneakers, pink ribbons, pink pants, and
a pink T-shirt that Lulu had to—she
desperately had to—say something.

(But before Lulu speaks, *I'd* like to say
that if these transformations seem kind
of impossible—and I'll be among the first
to admit that they do—it's because we do

not know the tricks of the trade. Spy craft can make anyone look shorter or taller; younger or older; female or male; animal, vegetable, or mineral. I may be writing this story, but the only folks here who know that stuff are Triple S, the former Head of All Spy Training, and Lulu, who is right now being trained.)

Except that maybe Lulu is about to stop being trained because—she cannot help herself—she simply HAS TO argue with Ms. Solinsky.

"A spy disguised as a pink and pigtailed

three-year-old? This is positively the dopiest, dumbest, stupidest thing I have ever heard in my life!"

Ms. Solinsky looked long and hard at Lulu. "And *this*," she said, "is gross insubordination"—a fancy way to say that you have seriously disobeyed me and you are doomed. "Since you have dared to question me, I hereby this minute resign as your spy trainer."

Lulu, in a panic, sunk to the floor and, actually begging on bended knees, asked Ms. Solinsky to give her one more chance.

And after a whole lot of "nos" from Ms. Solinsky and a whole lot of "please-please-please-please-pleases" from Lulu, Ms. Solinsky relented and said to Lulu, "I've already invested a great deal of time in your training. And therefore I will give you one more chance. I will also offer the following explanations, after which I will never again explain anything, and you never again will argue or complain."

Ms. Solinsky proceeded to explain:

"If you wanted to put a spy in a playground or preschool or day-care center, who's the LEAST suspicious person you could pick? The least suspicious person would be a little girl in pigtails, equipped with a hidden camera and a recording device. Have I made my point? Don't answer. Of course I have."

Ms. Solinsky cleared her throat again.

"And in order to prepare you for the next disguise we're doing, so you won't lose control when you look at yourself in the mirror, consider this question: If the bad guy you wanted to spy on was meeting another bad guy somewhere out in the country, with open fields and not a tree in sight, what disguise could you wear that would let you—without their having a clue—listen to every single word they said?"

Lulu, instead of trying to answer, took a look in the mirror. Calmly gazing back at her was . . . a cow.

chapter sixteen

$\mathcal{B}y$ the end of Monday, Lulu had learned to disguise herself as anyone and anything. She had also learned to notice all the little mistakes and carelessnesses that would tip her off when someone else was disguised. On Tuesday, Lulu's class would be taking a field trip to a museum, encountering many people during the day. Lulu's spy assignment was to figure out which of these people were actually an in-disguise Ms. Solinsky.

Early on Tuesday morning, an eager
Lulu was up and dressed, confident that
she would ace her assignment. But after
she had startled the substitute teacher
and the driver of the bus by whispering,
"Gotcha. I know who you are!" when she
didn't, she realized that she wasn't that
great at Penetrate. Concentrating harder
and using the spy craft that she had been
taught, Lulu got better as the day went

on, catching Ms. Solinsky disguised as a
tour guide at the museum and a cashier
at the cafeteria. Her greatest moment of
triumph, however, came at the very end of
the afternoon, when she shrewdly figured
out that the dog that was sitting in front
of her house when she got home from

school—a mutt that had peed profusely
on her sneakers—was actually none other
than Ms. Solinsky.

"I am impressed," Ms. Solinsky told
Lulu. "But don't get carried away with
yourself. We'll see, tomorrow, how well
you do when I'm teaching you H and C—
Hacking and Codes."

chapter seventeen

Hacking, Ms. Solinsky explained, was sneaking into other people's computers—computers sending out messages (like Lulu asking Mabel to bring over cats, or bad guys plotting how to destroy the world) that you definitely weren't ever supposed to read. Codes were ways of writing your top-secret messages so secretly that, even when hackers read what you had written, they couldn't understand a single word.

Working with Lulu on Wednesday, Ms. Solinsky first taught her several nifty codes and then moved on to the tricks of hacking computers, solemnly explaining to her, "Hacking is wrong and not nice and against the law, but you need to learn how to do it to be a good spy."

"And I do want to be a good spy. I do!" said Lulu—and then she dug in and learned how to hack faster than she had learned anything else in her life.

"You've got a natural talent," Ms. Solinsky said to Lulu. "But don't use it except when you're an official spy. Because if you're hacking to find out if Henry likes you better than he likes Nora Kaplan, you probably won't appreciate the answer."

"I have no idea what you're talking about," Lulu told Ms. Solinsky, who patted her on her shoulder and replied, "You are *so* much better at hacking than at lying."

chapter eighteen

GFEDCBA,
Triple S has got to stay.
June or April, March or May,
Triple S has got to stay.
Oink or quack or moo or neigh,
Triple S has got to stay.
Austin, Boston, Santa Fe,
Triple S has got to stay.

Lulu was chanting her friendly new chant as she fell asleep that night, wondering what Ms. Solinsky would teach her next. After Repair and Restore, Disguise and Penetrate, Hacking and Codes, she hardly could wait for the lesson that Thursday would bring.

chapter nineteen

Back from school on Thursday, Lulu was met at the door by Sonia Sofia Solinsky, who said to her, "We must hurry. Your parents return tomorrow night. Which means we haven't much time for me to give you your final lesson in basic spy craft."

She explained that this final lesson involved several clues that she had hidden all over the house, with each clue leading onward to the next. If Lulu succeeded in following them—which wouldn't be easy to do—she would find, at the end, what the clues had been leading her to.

"Which is what?" Lulu asked. "Tell me, and I'll get started. I'll get started right now and be finished before bedtime."

"I wouldn't count on being done before bedtime," said Ms. Solinsky. "And you aren't permitted to know in advance what you'll find. In fact, this particular lesson, which ends each set of my spy-craft lessons, is known as"—HERE IT COMES, FOLKS! HERE IT COMES!—"MM, which stands for"—YES!—"Mysterious Mission."

(And *that*, I sincerely hope, takes care of *that*!)

MYSTERIOUS MISSION! Lulu totally loved it. And she knew without a doubt that she would succeed. Indeed, by now she was positive that she was the best spy-in-training that Sonia Sofia Solinsky—code name Triple S—had ever trained.

"Aren't I the best spy-in-training that you have ever trained?" Lulu asked Ms. Solinsky.

"Let's not get pushy," Ms. Solinsky replied. Then she sat Lulu down in the kitchen, fed her an early supper, and handed her—printed neatly on a note card—the clue to where she should look for her next clue:

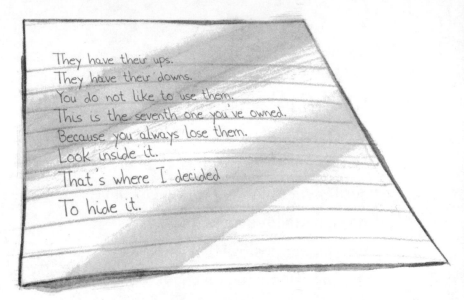

They have their ups.
They have their downs.
You do not like to use them.
This is the seventh one you've owned.
Because you always lose them.
Look inside it.
That's where I decided
To hide it.

Lulu narrowed her eyes as she read and re-read and then re-re-read the clue. She read it to herself, and she read it out loud. After which she turned to Ms. Solinsky and asked, in a quite snippy tone of voice, "What kind of dopey, dumb, stupid clue is *that*?"

Good grief—has Lulu forgotten total obedience?

"Excuse me," said Ms. Solinsky. "What did you say?"

Lulu, pulling herself together in the nick of time, replied, "Oh, I only just was saying that this clue is kind of confusing and was wondering if you could give me a little help."

"Careful attention to each of the words," Ms. Solinsky replied, "ought to give you all the help you need. And now I'm going up to my room and I don't wish to be disturbed. You're on your own."

At the top of the stairs, however, Ms. Solinsky stopped for a moment. "Inside it. Decided. Hide it," she said. "As you can see, my little spy-in-training, you're not the only one who knows how to rhyme."

You clever folks reading this story have doubtlessly already figured out what this clue was referring to. But it took Lulu quite a while to think of what goes up and down, and how she complains whenever her mom makes her use one, and that she had already lost a green one, a blue one, a plaid one, two flowered ones, and a frog one, making the yellow polka-dot one that hung in the front-hall closet her seventh . . . UMBRELLA.

Lulu rushed to that closet, reached
inside the hanging umbrella, and found
her next clue:

In something that rhymes with FOX
Is something that rhymes with EYES,
And taped to that second something
   is a clue.
You'll discover it all by yourself
On something that rhymes with ELF,
And there's even something for
   breakfast tomorrow too.

Two hours later, and getting close to her bedtime, Lulu came up—at last!— with BOX and PRIZE and SHELF and BREAKFAST CEREAL. Rummaging through the cereal *boxes* that stood on a *shelf* in the kitchen, she eventually pulled out of the Toasted Yummy Extra-Sugar Bits a purple plastic superhero—the *prize*—on the back of which was scotch-taped her next clue:

Inside of a shoe,
  near the toe,
Awaits what you
  next need to know.

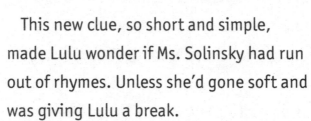

This new clue, so short and simple,
made Lulu wonder if Ms. Solinsky had run
out of rhymes. Unless she'd gone soft and
was giving Lulu a break.

But three hours later, and way way past
her bedtime, Lulu had found no clue in
the toe of a shoe, though she'd gone
through every shoe in her closet, as well
as every shoe of her mom's and her
dad's, and had even checked out
Ms. Solinsky's combat
boots. Disgusted,
discouraged, and

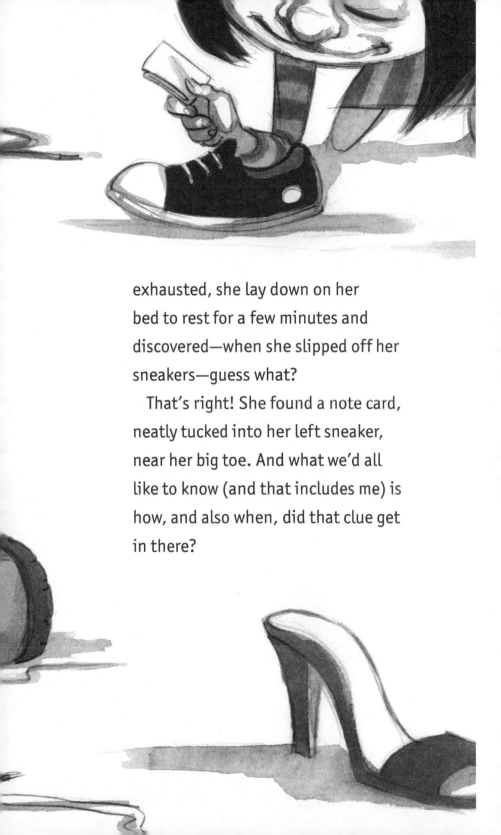

exhausted, she lay down on her
bed to rest for a few minutes and
discovered—when she slipped off her
sneakers—guess what?

That's right! She found a note card,
neatly tucked into her left sneaker,
near her big toe. And what we'd all
like to know (and that includes me) is
how, and also when, did that clue get
in there?

chapter twenty

Lulu couldn't wait to read the next clue, which went like this:

Open the striped curtain.
Raise the wooden blind.
Close the window all the way
And maybe you will find
What you are looking for.

There was only one room in the house with a striped curtain and wooden blind, and that was the bathroom next to Lulu's bedroom. And sure enough, when she opened and raised and closed, as she'd been instructed, there was a note card taped onto the window. Unfortunately, the note card said:

YES, MAYBE YOU WILL FIND IT.
AND MAYBE YOU WON'T.

Under that message, in smaller print, was another message:

So what do you think?
Is it under the sink?

Lulu looked under the bathroom sink, where she found another message:

NO, IT ISN'T!

Obviously, Ms. Solinsky was messing with her. Speaking out loud in the empty room, a disgusted Lulu announced, "I am not amused."
Below that message, however, was what seemed like a serious clue, a clue that Lulu was finding hard to read. She was finding it hard to read and even harder to understand

because her eyes kept closing with
exhaustion. It said:

In the living room, cleverly hidden,
Is the very last clue I have written,
Leading you directly to your goal.
You must rhyme what you need to
    find first
With the opposite of WORST,
On top of which is a thing that rhymes
    with HOLE.
And that thing that is rhyming with
    HOLE,
(As well as with POLE and with ROLL)
Is filled with things you can reach your
    hand in and take.
But although all these things rhyme
    with CUTE

(And BOOT, SUIT, TOOT, and LOOT)
The one that you are looking for is
   a fake.

   Lulu didn't think much of a poem
that had the utter nerve to rhyme
"written" and "hidden," but by now she
was so sleepy that she couldn't think
about anything but sleep. "I need to
go to bed. I have to get some sleep. I'll
get some sleep, and I'll wake up real

early tomorrow, and before I even eat breakfast, I'll figure this out."

Early on Friday morning, however, nothing got figured out. Lulu was still too sleepy and too fuzzy-headed. Besides which, this clue was really really HARD! (Maybe some of you DON'T think it's hard, in which case, smarty pantses, step right up and give us the answer right now. As for the rest of you—feel free to read on.)

Anyway, it was not until late in the morning—while Lulu was learning state capitals in her geography class—that CHEST (which rhymes with BEST, which is the opposite of WORST) and BOWL (which rhymes with HOLE and POLE and ROLL) all of a sudden popped into her brain, along with FRUIT (which rhymes with CUTE, plus BOOT, SUIT, TOOT, and LOOT). Then she had to wait for over four more maddening hours until—at last!—school was over and she could go home. And reach her hand down till she found—among the real FRUIT in the BOWL on the living room CHEST—an apple that was definitely fake. And read the clue that was hidden inside the fake apple. And follow that final clue to what she was looking for. It said:

Search no more. Search no more.
It's inside the chest, in the bottom
 drawer.

And it was!

chapter twenty-one

While Lulu was busy searching, Ms. Solinsky watched and waited, not saying a single word till Lulu plucked, from that bottom drawer, a silver disk that hung from a silver chain and upon which were boldly inscribed the letters MM. Then, standing at her tallest and straightest, Ms. Solinsky declared, "Mission accomplished." After which she carefully clasped the chain—with its gleaming disk—around Lulu's neck.

"This disk," she said, "hereby certifies that you have completed your first Mysterious Mission. My hearty congratulations, Double L."

Lulu was almost fainting, this time with joy. "You're giving me a code name? I've got my very own code name? From now on everyone calls me Double L?"

"I'm afraid I must remind you," Ms. Solinsky coldly replied, "that this is what's known as a covert operation. And covert means secret, undercover, hush-hush. You may not tell anyone—ANYONE; unless they're a fellow spy—your code name or that you're being trained in spy craft. And you'll need to remove that disk from your neck before anybody sees it, and put it away where nobody ever will."

LOOT). Then she had to wait for over
four more maddening hours until—at
last!—school was over and she could go
home. And reach her hand down till she
found—among the real FRUIT in the BOWL
on the living room CHEST—an apple that
was definitely fake. And read the clue
that was hidden inside the fake apple.

and all the kids at school, and Harry Potter"—she meant the other Harry Potter—"and my mom and my dad and Mr. B and . . . everyone?"

Ms. Solinsky began unclasping Lulu's silver chain. "We'll do it my way, or I take back your disk. Furthermore, I'll deny whatever you say about me, or you, being a spy. I'll swear that you're making it up, that you're telling lies, that you're imagining things. And I'll say it so many times that very soon your reputation will be . . . dog poop."

Ms. Solinsky looked at her watch. "Your parents," she said, "will be here in a couple of hours. You'd better decide what you are going to do."

There was a heavy silence in the living room. Lulu silently stared at Ms. Solinsky.

Ms. Solinsky silently stared back. Ten, fifteen, twenty, twenty-five minutes went by before they even started talking. And it wasn't until a few seconds before Lulu's mom and her dad were due home, that Lulu and Ms. Solinsky cut a deal.

Lulu, much as she hated it, swore never to mention her spy training or her code name, and promised to hide her disk in a safe place. Ms. Solinsky swore to train Lulu in spy craft whenever Lulu's mom and her dad went away. She also solemnly promised that when Lulu grew up and applied for a job as a spy, she'd write a letter saying nice things about her. Unless Lulu didn't deserve having nice things said about her. Or unless Lulu changed her mind and decided she'd rather be president of the United States.

But then Lulu's parents came home and almost ruined everything!

Rushing through the door and dropping their suitcases on the floor, they threw their arms around Lulu and started sobbing.

"Oh, my precious! My darling! My treasure!" wailed her weeping mom. "We missed you so very much! We hardly could stand it!"

"Oh, pumpkin. Oh, sweet pea!" her dad said, hugging her tight and soaking her shoulder with his hot tears. "It was awful being without you. We will never, never, ever do this again!"

Lulu was instantly on alert. "Do what again?" she demanded.

Her parents answered together. "We will never go away without you. Never!"

Lulu was shocked beyond shocked. This was a nightmare! A disaster! A catastrophe! She felt that she was about to lose her

mind! How would Ms. Solinsky be able to
train her to be a spy if her parents were
never going to leave her behind?

"You HAVE to, you've GOT to, you NEED

to take more vacations!" Lulu shouted. "You need some private, grown-ups-only time. You've got to go away a lot, and I will be just fine being babysat by DARLING Ms. Solinsky."

Lulu was now jumping up and down—and although it wasn't a tantrum, it was close—shouting, "Go! You have to go! Go! Go! Go!"

Lulu's mom and her dad were dazed and perplexed and completely confused and full of questions: What was going on here? What was she saying? Why was she acting in this peculiar way? Hadn't she, only a week ago, carried on most unpleasantly when they told her that they were going away without her? So why was she now insisting that she WANTED them to go away without her?

"Lulu, sweetie . . . ," her mom began.

"Lulu, honey . . . ," her dad began.

"What's gotten into you?" they asked together.

And Lulu, looking first at her mom and then at her dad, replied, "I guess I'm just an extremely difficult child."

chapter twenty-two

You won't be surprised to hear that after at least an hour of quite intense discussion, Lulu—as she so often did—got her way. This meant persuading her mom and her dad (though they swore they would miss her to pieces) to go off on lots of trips and vacations without her.

It also meant making them promise that
whenever they left town, they'd put her
in the care of Ms. Solinsky. Who, to their
bewilderment, seemed to have won their
daughter's undying affection. And who,
looking great in stiletto heels, loose hair,
and a slinky blue dress (she only wore the
uniform to intimidate extremely difficult
kids) was saying good-bye to everyone and
rushing off for a date with Harry Potter.

· · ·

And so, from that time on, Triple S came
to stay—several times a year—with Double
L, giving her lessons in spy craft, except
when she needed to be disciplined for
too much arguing and too little obeying.
For Lulu, you won't be surprised to
hear, continued to be difficult, though
not as extremely as she used to be. And
whenever she was, she was handed a little
toothbrush and a bucket of soapy water
and told to scrub the steps in front of her
house.

What made Lulu keep being difficult
was her absolute conviction that she
was the greatest spy-in-training ever.
And though, no doubt about it, she was
truly gifted and talented, she constantly
got into trouble because she constantly
wanted to do too much too soon.

Like trying to wreck, then Restore and
Repair, that tree by her bathroom window.

(Except that because Lulu's wrecking was so much better than her restoring, it required all of Ms. Solinsky's spy-craft skills to rescue the poor tree.)

Or like trying to Disguise herself as a helicopter. (It took Ms. Solinsky less than two seconds to Penetrate Lulu's disguise because most helicopters do not wear knee socks.)

Or like trying to Hack—imagine! The nerve!—into Ms. Solinsky's computer. (Except that when she did, she found that every single item of information—including some personal e-mails from Harry Potter—had been transcribed into an unbreakable Code.)

Or like trying to create a Mysterious Mission, complete with clues, for Ms. Solinsky to figure out and follow. (But

daughter's undying affection. And who, looking great in stiletto heels, loose hair, and a slinky blue dress (she only wore the uniform to intimidate extremely difficult kids) was saying good-bye to everyone and rushing off for a date with Harry Potter.

. . .

And so, from that time on, Triple S came to stay—several times a year—with Double L, giving her lessons in spy craft, except when she needed to be disciplined for too much arguing and too little obeying. For Lulu, you won't be surprised to

fact, she was feeling extremely proud of the stuff she had tried to do, even though it hadn't exactly worked out. In fact, she was feeling quite positive that even though she might not be good enough YET, she surely would be much more than good enough SOON.

However, she continued—in the interest of not making trouble—to hang her head.

Ms. Solinsky, who knew very well how to tell a truly embarrassed girl from a fake one, gave Lulu an oh-so-understanding smile.

After which she presented her, as she would for years to come, with a toothbrush and a bucket of soapy water.

The

End

Judith Viorst

is the author of many books for children, including the classic *Alexander and the Terrible, Horrible, No Good, Very Bad Day* and its sequels. She lives with her husband, Milton, in Washington DC.

Lane Smith

is the author and illustrator of the books *Grandpa Green*; *It's a Book*; and *John, Paul, George & Ben*. He has appeared on the *New York Times* Best Illustrated Children's Books of the Year list four times and has been a Caldecott Honoree. He lives with book designer Molly Leach in rural Connecticut, and can be visited at lanesmithbooks.com.

Kevin Cornell

Kevin Cornell draws from his intergalactic command base located in Philadelphia, Pennsylvania. Some of his most successful Earth missions include illustrating *Mustache!* and *Count the Monkeys* by Mac Barnett, and *The Trouble with Chickens* by Doreen Cronin. Make first contact with him at kevskinrug.com!